The *Earl's* Conquest

A Prequel to
An Unwavering Trust

by

L.L. Diamond

The Earl's Conquest
By L.L. Diamond

Published by L.L. Diamond
Copyright ©2015 LL Diamond

Cover and internal design © 2015 L.L. Diamond
Cover design by L.L. Diamond/Diamondback Covers
Cover Art: Elisabeth Louise Vigée Le Brun, Madame Grand
Source: Courtesty Met Museum Open Access (CC0)

ISBN-10: 0996789111
ISBN-13: 978-0-9967891-1-0

Facebook: https://www.facebook.com/LLDiamond
Twitter: @LLDiamond2
Blog: http://lldiamondwrites.com/
Austen Variations: http://austenvariations.com/

Other works by L.L. Diamond include:

Rain and Retribution
A Matter of Chance
An Unwavering Trust
The Earl's Conquest
Particular Intentions
Particular Attachments

Unwrapping Mr. Darcy
It's Always Been You
It's Always Been Us
It's Always Been You and Me
Undoing

To Brandon and our children, who will probably never read Jane Austen because of my craziness. I love you and thank you for putting up with my obsession!

Chapter 1

With a hand to her bulging abdomen, Elizabeth Darcy clenched her teeth at the tightening of the muscles in her belly. Grandmamma was correct when she said the next confinement might be different than Thomas'. The excruciating back pain she had endured with her son did not plague her as before, yet whilst Thomas was worth the trial, she had prayed the experience would not be repeated.

"Am I allowed to send for the midwife or will you continue to profess you are not labouring?"

She took a deep breath and released it, her free hand relinquishing its firm grasp of the bedclothes. "I wanted to be certain before you inconvenienced Mrs. Hewett this time."

Fitzwilliam gave a low growl as he cuddled her back to his chest, enfolding her in his arms. His warm breath tickled her cheek as he pressed a kiss to her ear. "I cannot help but be cautious—especially with the long carriage ride you endured in your condition!"

"I am not faulting your care but justifying the reason I have denied matters until now."

His splayed hand cradled her swollen belly. "It is so hard. Are you in a great deal of discomfort?"

Elizabeth caressed the back of his hand. "Thus far, it has been more an annoyance than pain, but the last pinched a bit."

His palm cupped her cheek, and he turned her head in his direction. "No more arguments. I intend to send for Mrs. Hewett.

"I have no intention of disagreeing with you."

"Truly?" Her husband's raised eyebrows and wide eyes displayed his surprise; however, he did not tarry, and with a swiftness that necessitated her bracing herself on her side, he jumped from the bed to check the corridor.

After a passing footman was dispatched to notify Mrs. Reynolds, Fitzwilliam returned to sit at her side. A look Elizabeth had not witnessed since the birth of Thomas fixed upon his face. She reached out to grasp his hands in her own.

"I will be well—*we* will be well. You must believe it will be so."

He swallowed heavily as he dropped his head to her shoulder. "I do not know what I would do if I were to lose you."

Her eyes burned at his heartfelt admission, and she lifted his head so their eyes met. "I have no intention of leaving, Fitzwilliam Darcy!"

"It is impossible to make such promises." His expression was so open and so child-like, seeking reassurance.

"I may have no control over what will happen, yet I can promise to fight with all I have to remain. God will have to prise me from this life as long as you are here."

She tensed with the next pain, grasping his hands as the intensity increased. When the episode was over, her husband released an exhale, which made her chuckle.

"You would faint from holding your breath if you remained."

Her heart ached at a thought, and she drew his head back so they were eye to eye. "I require a promise from you."

His brow furrowed. "I will promise you all you desire."

She shook her head. "I need nothing so grand. I assure you." She entwined her fingers with his and gave a gentle squeeze. "I need you to swear that should the worst ever happen."

A small gasp gave her pause, but he never averted his eyes from hers. "What would you wish of me?"

"I desire nothing more than for you to remain amongst the living. Thomas and any future children we have will require you to be strong for them. I would not have you turn your back on them due to your grief."

A knock on the door caused them both to start, and she bid them enter. Fitzwilliam's eyes did not leave her even as Elizabeth greeted Grandmamma.

"I heard the midwife was summoned, and thought you might be in want of my hand to hold. I see you have Fitzwilliam, though we know he will not endure your temper when the time comes."

Elizabeth smiled as her husband bent to kiss her reverently. When he lifted and touched his forehead to hers, she clenched his hands with her own. "I love you. You must believe we will be well."

He nodded and bestowed a long kiss between her eyebrows. With one last brush of his lips to her hairline, he pressed his temple to hers, his warm breath caressing her ear. "I do swear. You would never leave my heart, but I would do as you ask."

Before she could thank him, he withdrew, strode with purpose to the door, and departed.

"He is more emotional than when you were in your confinement with Thomas," observed the dowager.

"Fitzwilliam had little time to consider the situation at hand the night Thomas was born. One moment, I was merely having back pains during dinner, the next, I was ushered to my chambers, and my waters broke."

Grandmamma gave a nod of agreement as she took her seat beside Elizabeth. "Your bond has also grown in the last few years. You will find as your marriage continues to grow and mature that your heart will bind itself to his in ways you had never conceived possible."

The elder woman spoke from experience—her own experience of course. The entire family was aware how much Grandmamma grieved the loss of her husband. He may have passed from this Earth years prior, but Grandmamma's love for him never diminished; she still adored him with her entire being.

Elizabeth took her grandmother's hand and encased it in hers. "Tell me of how you came to wed your husband."

The dowager's eyebrows lifted, and Elizabeth grinned. "Please?"

"You cannot want to hear that story," the beloved lady demurred with a tinge of pink in her cheeks. "Such a sentimental tale can only be of importance to the individuals involved."

Taken aback, Elizabeth raised herself onto her forearm. "You have never spoken of the courtship you shared, have you?"

"There were those who knew what transpired that autumn. Most have passed away now, but whilst I treasured my memories, I never thought my son would take an interest in the tale." She fingered the wedding bands on Elizabeth's finger. "I told Anne once, but I did not tell her all."

"Why not? Did she not enjoy hearing her parent's love story?"

Grandmamma gave a soft smile. "Anne was diverted indeed, but I feared telling her certain parts. I was so headstrong and impertinent as a young woman." She gave a rueful chuckle. "I believe I loved Gerald from the first moment of our acquaintance, but I fought my attachment. He was taken with me as well, deciding swiftly to pursue me—I required some convincing to be persuaded to his way of thinking.

"Yet he did win your hand." Her stomach clenched painfully, and she drew in a long, slow breath in an attempt to withstand the sensation.

"You truly wish for me to bore you?"

Elizabeth shook her head and sank back into the pillows. "No, I believe I will find your tale amusing, and I insist you tell me all."

"You are being quite demanding!" exclaimed Grandmamma whilst she attempted to maintain a serious expression.

As she bit her bottom lip, Elizabeth lifted one shoulder. "I am in my confinement, so I am certain you will excuse my impertinence."

"I would not be too certain, but I will bow to your wishes this once."

"I had hoped you might." Elizabeth's heart gave a quiver. Grandmamma alluded to the courtship between her and the earl often but never provided detail. The story was certain to be a romantic one, yet Grandmamma never disclosed the entirety—just enough to arouse one's curiosity.

"Youth is easily deceived because it is quick to hope."[1]

"There are only two bequests we can hope to give our children. One of these is roots, the other, wings."[2]

"You read entirely too much, Elizabeth Darcy."

Elizabeth giggled and lifted one eyebrow.

"Oh, very well. But I still claim that the tale will put you to sleep."

Elizabeth's gaze never wavered.

"I suppose I should start from the beginning, then?"

With a wide grin, Elizabeth situated herself so she was as comfortable as could be whilst she awaited the next pain.

"I first met Gerald in September of 1757…"

[1] Aristotle
[2] Johann Wolfgang von Goethe

Chapter 2

1757

Miss Rebecca Fairchild took in the view of majestic Warrington Hall as she trod with care along the side of the soggy hill. The home appeared quiet, yet, despite its outward appearance, a house party took place within the manor. The dinner she was to attend that evening with her family was in honour of the guests. She stopped to stare, tilting her head as she appraised the grand structure.

Warrington, which belonged to the Earl of Sudbury, was known to be the largest estate in the county, yet the current earl had not entertained until his recent marriage. Rebecca had never stepped foot inside. Would the interior be overdone and uselessly fine, or did the new countess redecorate the house in a simple but elegant style?

A sigh escaped her lips. How she wished the ball were tonight rather than the dinner! She should not be so particular, but she enjoyed dancing and doubted a formal dinner party in honour of the Earl's guests would include a dance.

With a smile, she began to hum a tune as she turned and stepped according to a familiar pattern. Her imaginary partner led her effortlessly until her foot slipped on a patch of loose earth and her rear smarted upon contact with the ground.

"Oh dear!" she burst out with a laugh.

Once she was back upon her feet, she pivoted her torso to assess if there was any damage to the back of her gown, finding a large swath of dirt from her hip to her ankle.

She grimaced. "Mother will not be pleased." She attempted to brush the filth from her skirt, but bit her bottom lip when the muck smeared. "Oh no!"

Although she only ruined perhaps one gown a year, her mother would be apoplectic. Her father, on the other hand, would chuckle, kiss her on the forehead, and say, "Try to be more careful in the future, sweetling." He never lost his temper, but he also still called her sweetling—an endearment more appropriate for a child than a young woman of her one and twenty years.

She brushed her hands together in an attempt to clean some of the filth from them, a wide grin adorning her face as she considered the upcoming scene at home. How her mother would rant and rave! Those objections, however, would fall upon deaf ears since Rebecca did not give a fig about what others said.

A low laugh came from behind her, and she whipped around, her foot once again meeting the spot of mud and causing her to plop with a less than graceful thud to the ground.

"Oh bother!" she muttered.

As she made to rise, a large, gloved hand appeared before her. "Please forgive me for startling you. I should have departed straight away when I first noticed you dancing, but I did not."

Rebecca accepted the hand, which pulled her from the ground. Once on her feet, she examined the new damage. "Has anyone ever informed you that it is impolite to spy on someone who believes themselves to be alone?"

Her voice held bite, but who did this man think he was! He should not have been watching her so!

"You are correct, of course."

She gave a huff and turned towards the man with every intention of flaying him with her tongue, but those intemperate words were forgotten when her eyes set upon his. He was not a servant or a tenant farmer, but a gentleman—and a handsome one at that! He was older than she, but those eyes!

His lip gave a slight quirk as he dipped in a brief bow. "As I said, I do apologise for disturbing your solitary reverie. If you can assure me you are not injured, I shall bother you no longer."

She shook her head. "You are not a bother." The words she uttered registered and her face burned in mortification. "I thank you for ensuring I am unhurt. I vow that other than my wounded pride, I am well."

His low chuckle stirred the butterflies within her stomach and she shuddered.

"You must be cold." His voice rang of concern as his hand brought a flask from his pocket. "A sip of this will set you to rights."

Rebecca gave the open lid a sniff and wrinkled her nose. "This will warm me?"

After a reassuring nod, she tipped the container for a taste, but the liquid flowed into her mouth faster than she anticipated and burned! It singed her throat, her chest, and her stomach was now exceedingly warm. She began to cough, and he grasped the flask from her hand.

"That was a bit more than a sip. Brandy is not meant to be gulped."

"I assure you, sir," she rasped. "I had not intended to take more than you indicated." With one last clearing of her throat, she straightened her posture and stood tall. "I thank you for your aid, but I should return home."

Her eyes never left the gentleman as she took her first step—into the same damp spot as before. His strong hand seized her arm as she slipped once more. "You will ride my horse, and I shall take you home."

"It is not necessary. I do not live far."

"That may very well be, but if you have had too much brandy, I shall not be responsible for you injuring yourself after I depart."

How dare he insinuate she was incapable of walking on her own!

She put her hands upon her hips. "I am not at all affected by the contents of your flask, I promise you. I can make my way without aid."

Despite her objections, his hand remained upon her elbow as he guided her towards his large stallion. "Sir! I do not require the use of your horse. I prefer to walk."

Her protests fell upon deaf ears as his hands grasped her waist and lifted her atop the saddle. She glared down to his amused eyes. "Are you in the habit of ignoring the express wishes of all young ladies?"

His amused grin revealed a single dimple. "No, I am not. Only those audacious enough to overindulge on my brandy."

"I may have had one gulp," she defended. "I hardly imbibed some great quantity as you seem to believe."

"Nevertheless, I will ensure you reach your home without incident."

"I must protest. I have no intention of being escorted by a stranger."

An amused twinkle in his green eyes accompanied by a lopsided grin merely served to make her more irritated, but before she could so much as give an indignant huff, he placed his hand atop the stallion's mane.

"It is not as if I can harm you whilst you are atop my horse, and you shall have the reins whilst I lead him by the portion near the bit. You could escape with ease should you feel imperilled."

She peered down to the strips of well-tended leather that she held within her grasp. He was correct. She had the advantage and could not only escape, but could also render him without his mount should she wish it.

A resigned sigh escaped her lips. "Very well." She lifted her arm and pointed to the trail through the field before them. "The path is straight ahead."

With a grin, he began to walk as she maintained a fierce grip upon the reins. Their pace was never quick or such that she might fall, so after a time, she relaxed and studied the gentleman from behind.

He was certainly tall, with thick, sandy brown hair and broad shoulders; his dark topcoat and buckskin breeches becoming to his bearing and figure.

Without warning his head turned, and he peered back. "May I ask where I am escorting you?"

"My father's estate is called Marysden." She gestured toward a cluster of trees, and he made the appropriate turn.

"I believe I have heard it mentioned since my arrival in the neighbourhood. Is your family invited to the ball at Warrington a week hence?"

"Yes, sir. We are." Was there a reason for such questions other than general curiosity? She was not particularly happy with his officiousness in the situation, regardless of whether or not he was being a gentleman.

"So, you were indeed practicing your dancing for..."

"Sir, I know how to dance. I simply enjoy the activity and was taking pleasure in the weather and the solitude—until you arrived."

"You mean until you slipped."

"I would not have fallen a second or even a third time had you not arrived, sir!"

Another chuckle could be heard over the sound of the horse's hooves and his boots against the forest floor. "Are you always so forthright in your opinions?"

Her behaviour gave her pause. She was upset with him, to be certain, but had she been rude? Mrs. Mallory often attempted to curb her sharp tongue, but with little effect. Of course, her father loved her for her wit; she would not alter herself to suit society's standards. She might be polite and proper in company, yet she could not help the occasional bold remark.

"I appreciate honesty," she conceded, "but I do not speak every thought that comes to mind."

"Honesty is an admirable quality."

She pulled back on the reins. "Would you please stop here? I would prefer to proceed on foot. I assure you I am well enough for the short distance remaining."

He pointed between the trees. "Are the chimneys ahead Marysden?"

"Yes."

With a turn and a step, he lifted her down from the saddle as though she weighed less than a feather. "You do not want to cause a commotion by having a strange man accompany you home?"

"It might be difficult to explain why I am in your company when I know naught of you—not even your name."

His dimple appeared with a wide grin. "I would prefer to defer that exchange until we are properly introduced." A swift move saw him seated atop his horse as he continued to smile in a mischievous manner. "Do you foresee a problem with my request?"

She tilted her head and raised her hand to shield her eyes from the sunlight filtering through the trees. "I suppose not. Although, it seems an odd thing to ask."

"You should go. I wish to wait until I am certain you are safe, and I have been gone for too long. I must return to Warrington."

She rolled her eyes and gave a swift curtsy. "Good day, sir." With a hasty turn towards her home, she began to walk.

"You will not thank me for coming to your assistance?"

As she continued, she called over her shoulder. "But I would not have required your aid had you not interrupted me."

His low laugh resonated in the clearing, which prompted a small smile to cross her face. She stepped from the trees into the back garden of Marysden, and made her way to the door to the kitchens. Before she entered, she peered back to where he sat upon his horse, waiting, and held up a hand. He reciprocated the gesture, but did not ride away.

With a deep breath, she pushed the door forward and entered into the warm kitchen. A breeze wafted in from the window, but it did little to help with the overwhelming heat emanating from the fire and the stove.

"Miss Rebecca! There you are!" cried the cook. "Your mother has been threatening to send out the stable hands to find you!"

Chapter 3

Rebecca started at the immediate reprimand, but then, rolled her eyes. "I have yet to do anything, and I am to receive a scolding. However have I managed it?"

Mrs. Mallory, the housekeeper, came bustling through the entry. "I would watch your insolence if I were you, miss. The missus is on a right tear today."

"Well, if you hear her tell it, I am the reason Sarah is still unwed when we all know very well that it is Sarah's demeanour that harms her own prospects."

"What you think and what you should say are two different matters," scolded Mrs. Mallory until the cook startled them both with a gasp.

"Miss Rebecca, what *did* you do to your gown?"

The housekeeper's eyes widened, and she moved around Rebecca to see her muddied skirt. "We will have to get you changed before your mother sees that! Let us go. We do not have a second to lose!"

With a tut, Mrs. Mallory ushered her up the servants stairs to her rooms and pulled the bell; however, rather than wait for the maid she shared with Sarah, Mrs. Mallory began unbuttoning the back of Rebecca's gown to help her herself.

Mary appeared soon after the bell and stopped short upon entering the room. "Oh, miss! What have you done?"

Rebecca giggled. "I slipped in a bad patch of mud it seems."

"I do not know if I can remove it." Mary picked up the gown to study the stain. "How will I hide this from the mistress? She will wonder why you have only three morning gowns remaining."

"Stop fretting!" admonished Mrs. Mallory. "Help me get her changed before Mrs. Fairchild..."

Mrs. Mallory halted in mid-sentence and stared at the door. Rebecca followed the housekeeper's eyes to her mother, who stood in the doorway with her lips drawn to a fine line. "I was headed to my rooms to retrieve a book, and I was certain I heard your voices."

Her eyes narrowed as she studied Rebecca. "Why were you so long this morning? I forbade you from spending the entire morning out of doors, and you disobeyed my wishes. I have half a mind to prevent you from attending the dinner party this evening, but your father would never allow it."

Her mother speared Mary with a penetrating gaze.

"Mary, would you please fetch my gown?"

The maid jumped, glanced to Rebecca, and frantically began to nod. "Yes, miss. Right away."

The suspicious looks moved to herself and Mrs. Mallory before her mother turned to depart, pausing when she had pivoted half-way. "Rebecca, once you are dressed, you will attend me in the drawing room. Do you understand?"

"Yes, ma'am."

When her mother exited, the ladies remaining gave a collective exhale as the door clicked shut.

Mary came bustling back in from the dressing room, Rebecca's pale apricot silk draped over her arm. "At least she did not notice the gown! It may be a matter of time before she does, but I would prefer it if she were in one of her better moods."

Rebecca could not suppress a small snort. "Since Sarah is unlikely to become betrothed, an improvement of her mood is doubtful."

"You should not speak so of your sister," chided Mrs. Mallory.

"Why? When it is common knowledge about the neighbourhood?"

14

"Whilst that may be true, it is not charitable as you are well aware."

The housekeeper peered over the tops of her spectacles, and Rebecca sighed. "She may not be the loving sister I always wished to have, but I would never say such things to our friends or at a party."

"I am glad to hear it."

When the housekeeper and the maid had her set to rights, Rebecca sought out her mother in the drawing room, unsurprised to find Sarah seated and embroidering a design on a cushion.

"I am here as you requested, Mama."

Her mother set down her pen and rose from the escritoire. "Please have a seat. I would like to review my expectations of your behaviour at tonight's party."

"Am I not supposed to expose my ankles or bat my eyelashes to the gentlemen present?"

Sarah scoffed. "Your attempts at humour are not amusing in the least and show a decided lack of respect for my mother."

With a raised hand, her mother silenced the scolding of her elder sister. "I appreciate your defence, dear, but I am accustomed to Rebecca's inappropriate humour." Her attention returned to Rebecca and that same hand moved to point towards her youngest daughter's chest. "Your father may insist upon your attendance tonight, but he cannot prevent me from punishing you over the course of the next week. Do not try my patience!"

Rebecca's teeth bit the inside of her lip in a vain attempt to remain quiet. She had no desire to begin an argument between her parents. Her father would never sanction her mother's discipline, but the last row had her mother in a foul mood for a fortnight at least!

A satisfied smile lit her mother's face. "Ah, I see I have struck a chord with you. Good." She sat in the closest chair to Rebecca and folded her hands primly in her lap.

"I have heard from Mrs. Easton that the party at Warrington includes the Earl of Matlock, who was widowed nigh on two years ago. He would be a splendid match for Sarah, so I expect you to be on your best behaviour."

Her mother's eyes bore into her own, and Rebecca clenched her hands together and dug her teeth further into her lip. She was not inappropriate by any means! Perhaps a bit forthright, but she was not offensive and not an embarrassment.

"As a matter of fact, I believe it would be altogether better if you avoided the earl tonight and at the ball in a se'nnight as well as any gatherings where you may be in company together. Am I understood?"

"Yes, ma'am," she responded in a flat tone.

"Marrying the Earl of Matlock would be a tremendous coup. Imagine Sarah as a countess!"

The deeper voice of her brother, Aubrey interrupted, "I would not begin purchasing my sister's trousseau just yet, Mother." Aubrey stood in the doorway but after a moment, strode to the sofa.

The wide eyes and raised eyebrows, which composed her mother's feigned innocence, made Rebecca's insides roil. Her father and brother knew her mother's personality well, yet it did not keep the woman from pretending when the situation suited her.

"Sarah has all of the proper accomplishments, she is handsome, and she is a gentleman's daughter. I do not see why the earl would object."

"Papa and I have been invited to two hunting parties since Lord Matlock's arrival to Warrington. According to the talk amongst the men, he has ignored every young woman placed before him since his re-entry into society, and as we were shooting yesterday, he made mention of his late wife. I gather the marriage was not a happy one, and he will not marry again without careful consideration of the intended lady and their felicity together."

"Sarah is an amiable young lady. I am certain she would suit…"

A slight snort escaped, and her mother gave Rebecca a glare. Sarah would suit a viper. How could her mother assume she knew this gentleman's preferences without ever making his acquaintance?

Her brother sat as he shook his head. "Sarah would not satisfy his preferences, and I doubt he will look more than once in her direction."

"Then it is your job to ensure he considers your sister as his next wife."

"I will do no such thing," asserted Aubrey, setting his elbows upon his knees. "The earl is an amiable man, and despite our differences in rank and circumstance, he has treated me with nothing but respect and consideration. I will not do him the disservice of insinuating that he does not know his own mind."

"It is of no matter." Everyone's attention was drawn to Sarah, who had placed her embroidery upon her lap and now wore a smug smirk. "I do not require your aid. I will ensnare the earl myself."

Aubrey stood and towered over his mother and sister. "Know this, Sarah. I will advise father of this conversation. I will not call out the earl if you compromise your own reputation with him. He may be a man of honour, but I will not force him to sacrifice his happiness to ensure your own."

"You would ruin your beloved Rebecca in the process," spat Sarah like a little adder. Beneath all the false sweetness and sincerity lurked a nasty, spiteful woman of five and twenty. She had been passed over by most men, either because they saw through her and took her measure or because they learned of her true nature due to the gossip of their relations.

"Father and I would ensure Rebecca found a good husband if she ever wished it." Aubrey stood and made to leave, but her mother's voice halted his progress.

"Anything Rebecca wants Rebecca gets. One day you will marry and your wife may not appreciate your precious sister under her roof."

With an abrupt pivot, he levelled a heated stare at his mother. "I have no doubt the lady I wed will accept and love Rebecca as much as I do."

Aubrey stretched out his arm in her direction. "Come, Rebecca. I will take you to father directly."

Not one to question good fortune, Rebecca sprang from her seat and took her brother's arm, hurrying alongside him to her father's library.

Without knocking, her brother strode through the dark-stained oak door, garnering their father's attention. "Mother has decided Lord Matlock is Sarah's new conquest. I just interrupted her instructing Rebecca on her deportment and effective non-engagement of the earl."

Her father gave a resigned sigh and placed his pen in its holder. "I have attempted for years to rein her in, and she does not listen. She is frugal when it comes to our expenses, so I cannot threaten her allowance, which leaves me at a loss as to a solution that does not invite scandal upon us. If we could but have Rebecca wed, I would move with your mother and Sarah to the dower cottage. You could take over Marysden. But Rebecca could not remain without inciting talk amongst the neighbours." He gave her a wan smile. "I will not harm your prospects."

"I am unconcerned by my prospects, Papa. I have little in the way of a dowry, no lofty connections, and I have no interest in any of the eligible men of our acquaintance."

A chuckle drew her gaze to Aubrey. "I have friends from Cambridge."

"I am also not a prize mare to be auctioned to the highest bidder. I do not wish to be displayed to your friends."

Her father laughed and shook his head. "You are too stubborn, sweetling."

"I am exceedingly sorry if my spinsterhood ensures you the continued presence of my mother and my sister, but I abhor the preening and fawning of the marriageable ladies. I refuse to be anything other than myself."

"We would never ask you to be someone you are not," interjected her brother. "We would do no more than make introductions. Whether you further the acquaintance is your choice. I would never introduce you to a gentleman you would find a dullard."

"I know you would not." Her shoulders fell, and she choked back the burning of tears flooding her eyes. "I have always believed I would happen upon the man I was to marry. I cannot explain it, but I do not expect to make his acquaintance in a drawing room or at a ball. Moreover, I have never dreamed of being introduced to my future husband by my brother.

Aubrey's disappointment was etched upon his features and made her heart heavy with remorse. Her answer was not the one he wanted to hear.

"I will respect your wishes for now, Bec, but if you have not become betrothed by the Season, I will speak to a friend of mine who once offered to host my family for a month in London during that time. If he agrees, we will journey to Town."

"You just want me married, so you do not feel guilty when you wed Miss Abbot and bring her home to Marysden."

"You would never be relegated to the dower cottage."

His honest admission relieved the nervous churning in her stomach that began when the subject of her marriage prospects arose. If she did not find a husband, she would not be forced to accept a gentleman to escape the suffocating confines of the dower cottage with her mother and elder sister.

19

It was a welcome discovery indeed!

Chapter 4

The carriage was its usual crush as they journeyed to Warrington for the party. Of course, her mother and Sarah refused to allow their dresses to be crushed and creased by crowding all three ladies together, so rather, Rebecca sat opposite them, squeezed between her tall and well-statured father and brother. Not that she complained of the situation. The congestion of that side of the carriage was preferable to being in such close proximity to her mother and elder sister.

Her mother eyed Rebecca's new gown and gave a disdainful sniff as Rebecca smoothed a wrinkle in the fine material and diverted her eyes to once again study the colour and detail on the patterned overskirt.

The invitations for tonight's party and next week's ball had been a source of overwhelming excitement for the eldest ladies at Marysden. Her mother had insisted Sarah required new gowns for each event whilst Rebecca would wear one of her sister's gowns from the previous year; however, with Sarah's spiteful nature, the item she would pass to Rebecca would have a tear, whether already present or inflicted on purpose for the occasion.

It was Mrs. Mallory who heard her mistress' plans and informed Rebecca's father of the scheme afoot, yet rather than insisting her mother take her to the local seamstress, he had escorted her himself, insisting on the finest materials she had available.

The green silk she now wore was by far the most beautiful gown Rebecca had ever owned. For once, she was allowed to select the plate and the material, and she was exceedingly pleased with the result. She adored the line of the bodice, the ruffled and layered sleeves—an extravagance her mother only allowed in Sarah's wardrobe—and the skirt, which hung well on her figure.

Her father was so incensed that his wife would continue her attempts to sabotage his youngest daughter that he had not stopped with the gown. He also purchased new gloves and slippers to ensure she was well-dressed this evening.

Under his direction, the new garments had been a guarded secret until her entrance just prior to their departure, which sent her mother into a fit of anger. When it was apparent she would be relegated to Marysden for the evening if she continued her tirade, her mother ceased her complaints, but bestowed a gimlet eye to her youngest daughter whenever she was afforded the opportunity.

Rebecca bit her lip to suppress a grin. What would her mother say upon seeing her least favourite daughter's new ball gown?

Once they had arrived at Warrington, her brother stepped from the coach, but handed her out before her father followed, aiding her mother and Sarah.

The grand house was lit for the event and golden light glowed from every window as a prim servant awaited them near the doors to usher them inside. Upon their entrance, they were greeted by the Earl and Countess of Sudbury, who proceeded to introduce them to their other guests for the evening.

As Lord Sudbury named each member of her family, Rebecca scanned the room, her eyes halting on a familiar insufferable grin upon a familiar face. She managed to contain her gasp of surprise as she recognised none other than the gentleman from that morning!

During their earlier conversation, he had indicated he was aware of her family, so he had known of their invitation, which *certainly* explained his decided lack of shock at her arrival. What arrogant presumption!

She continued to stare in his direction until a movement by her brother distracted her. With an internal groan, she dipped a brief curtsy. Whose introduction had she missed?

"Why are you so distracted?" whispered Aubrey in her ear once everyone began to mill about the room. A servant brought glasses of wine, and she took one, sipping the vintage to quell the nervous anxiety that had erupted within her.

"It is a long story. I will tell you all, but not here and not now."

A low, familiar voice drew her attention. "Good evening, Fairchild. Will you do me the honour of introducing me to the lady on your arm?" Her head jolted to the gentleman from this morning, standing directly before her.

Aubrey wore a rare, proud expression when he gestured towards her. "Lord Matlock, I would like you to make the acquaintance of my youngest sister Miss Rebecca Fairchild.

"Rebecca, this gentleman is the Earl of Matlock."

It took all the restraint she could muster to temper her reaction. This man was the Earl of Matlock? The one Sarah and her mother wished to ensnare? A part of her felt pity for him, but she found him altogether too unnerving for all of her to pity him.

"I am pleased to make your acquaintance, Lord Matlock." She curtsied as he gave a bow, and returned his attention to her brother.

"I believe I rode close by your home today, Fairchild. I could see the chimneys through the trees."

Her eyes widened and her teeth began to gnaw on her bottom lip.

"You must have been close! You should have stopped by for a game of chess or to speak with father. I daresay he would have enjoyed the company."

Her brother's face was happy and animated, although he was unaware of the earl's little game to discompose her. She riled at the man's presumption. Perhaps he did deserve Sarah. What was she thinking? No one deserved to be saddled with a younger version of her mother.

"I considered doing just that, but I was concerned I would be intruding. You mentioned having sisters, and ladies are always busy the day of a party with situating their gowns and planning their hair."

Aubrey chuckled. "My mother and Sarah would have been occupied arranging matters, but Rebecca often takes a long ramble on mornings such as this."

She found the earl's eyes upon her once again. "You do?"

"Yes, sir. I do not care for the hectic air of the house on days such as today. I much prefer the outdoors."

Despite his scheme, his countenance was warm and not at all mischievous. "I do much the same, Miss Rebecca. It is precisely the reason I took a long ride this morning, and when I returned, I handled my business affairs, which kept me out of the household's way."

An odd sensation prompted her to look to his side where she caught her elder sister spearing her with a hateful glare capable of giving most children a fright.

She diverted her attention and opened her mouth to speak; however, before she could utter a single sound, dinner was announced, so she clamped her jaw shut.

The earl gave a brief bow. "If you will excuse me."

Her eyes followed the earl as he offered his arm to another young lady. They then followed their hosts to the dining room where Aubrey escorted her to her chair before going in search of his own.

As she waited for the remainder of her party to be seated, the place card beside hers caused her to startle. She was to be seated by Lord Matlock? Oh no, that would not do! Would he bait her for the entire dinner to make her angry? Then what of Sarah? She would be livid!

The gentleman himself appeared a moment later and took his seat with a grin. "It seems we are to be dining partners tonight. I hope you do not mind my company?"

She gave a small shake of her head. "Of course not, my lord."

The meal commenced and a conversation began, so she was caught unprepared when his voice spoke low from beside her. "I hope you will forgive me for not introducing myself this morning. As we were hunting a few days ago, your brother spoke of how close the two of you are. When I realised who you were, and that you would be attending tonight, I suppose I wanted to once again take you by surprise."

She rested her hand, which held her spoon, beside her place setting. He could be the most infuriating man! "I, on the other hand, would have preferred a bit of warning. You have no idea the trouble your little introduction will cause me."

His forehead creased in thought. "I do not see why. There was nothing untoward in the interaction. We were in a drawing room full of people."

With a sigh, she glanced around to be certain the remainder of the table was deep in conversation. Her mother was observing her with narrowed eyes, but she returned to the earl's concerned gaze.

"I would not speak so under normal circumstances, but in this case, I feel I must warn you. Upon learning of your presence from the local gossip, my sister has decided to set her cap at you."

"Indeed." With a lift of his eyebrows, he took a sip of his wine. "And her conquest bothers you?"

"No!" she hissed. "If you want to wed my sister, then that is your prerogative."

"Yet, you decided to warn me."

He wore that ridiculous quirk of the lips, and she bristled in response. "You may be insufferable, but my sister is not amiable or kind. I do not wish her upon any man or any woman for that matter."

His warm gaze studied her, and she tensed her hand to hide the slight shake she felt. Why did he insist upon staring at her so?

"I thank you for your warning." A pause allowed her to take a few bites of soup before she heard his voice speak even lower, if possible.

"Your sister and your mother do not appear pleased. Do they have reason to suspect our previous acquaintance?"

"No, I have not told a soul. I was warned to steer clear of you this evening and at the ball. Whilst I cannot control the seating arrangement, my mother and Sarah will be displeased at my conversing with you."

"Then, I will apologise now for any inconvenience our acquaintance may cause you at home."

Her eyes left the spoon and appraised his countenance. His manner was open and honest with no hint of deception or malice. She gave a small nod and returned to her food. A minute later, his voice interrupted her thoughts.

"Do you have any accomplishments beyond dancing?"

Insufferable man!

The last course was served, and Rebecca was about to have a colossal fit of nerves. The earl had proved himself an amiable dinner conversationalist—even if he was prone to the occasional impertinence. But who was she to criticise for a fault she owned to herself. On the other hand, it was her mother and sister who made her wary.

"Miss Rebecca, are you well?"

Her line of vision darted from the menacing stare of her sister to the earl's worried green orbs. "'Tis nothing. Please do not concern yourself."

He peered around the table, pausing upon Sarah, who, with a prompt head turn, feigned an interest in the person to her opposite side. "Your sister is angry due to our conversation."

She closed her eyes in mortification. "Yes, I have noticed."

As Lady Sudbury rose to lead the ladies to the withdrawing room, the earl rose and whispered in her ear as Rebecca stood. What was he about?

The lady patted the earl's arm and called for the women to follow, but upon reaching the hall, the countess took Rebecca's elbow. "Miss Rebecca, I have not had the opportunity to know you better this evening. I hope you will indulge me for a time."

How her jaw did not drop in shock was a mystery, yet she did not tarry or take the time to question her good fortune. The countess ushered Rebecca to the seat beside her on the sofa, and included her in the conversation until the men returned.

The earl found her upon his entrance, and his shoulders gave an almost imperceptible drop. He did not appear displeased, so he must have been relieved she appeared well. Indeed, she had been fretful of when the ladies separated, as she would be without the protection of her father and brother until the gentleman had finished their port and cigars.

Upon Aubrey's entrance, she begged to be excused from her present company, and wended her way through the party towards her brother until a hand grabbed her just below the elbow, forcing her to halt and turn to discover who impeded her progress. Her sister's ugly sneer gave her reason to jerk back, but Sarah dug her fingernails into the soft, tender flesh of the underside of her arm.

"Mother ordered you to steer clear of the earl."

Rebecca glanced in her brother's direction, but he was busy with Miss Abbot; he did not know of her predicament. With a swallow, she attempted to quell her nerves. They would not be of aid to her present situation.

"Lord Matlock requested the introduction, and I could hardly control the seating arrangements. Was I supposed to increase your chances of ensnaring the earl by snubbing him? If so, I will be certain to do so next time. He will no doubt be more inclined towards you after I ignore him."

Her sister's fingernails gave another painful dig, and Rebecca's eyes burned as she struggled to withhold her tears.

"You may be Father's favourite, but my mother will not stand for your insolence." In an abrupt motion, Sarah whipped around and strolled over to re-join their mother as she chatted with the wife of a neighbour.

Rebecca turned her arm and peered down to the angry cuts left from Sarah's fingernails, each oozing enough blood to mar the pristine white ruffles of her new gown if she allowed it. With careful movements, she removed her handkerchief from her reticule and placed it against the wounds in the hopes of saving the silk from a nasty stain.

Her father had spent more than was his wont because he wanted to give her something special. She would not allow Sarah to ruin it like she ruined anything Rebecca held dear to her heart.

Chapter 5

"Miss Rebecca..."

She started as the earl took her forearm. "Please remove the handkerchief."

"It is of no consequence," she whispered. "The bleeding will stop soon. I am certain of it."

He scanned the room and stopped a passing footman, who he spoke to in such a way she was unable to hear. Once he nodded the servant away, he gestured towards a door on the far side of the room.

"I want you to go through those doors. I have arranged for a maid to clean those cuts. In the meantime, I will notify your brother and your father, so they will not worry."

"I do not wish to be a bother, sir. I will continue on as I have."

"Nonsense. You will do as I say, or I will escort you myself."

His commanding tone bristled, and she stood fast, refusing to move. "Are you always so recalcitrant?"

"Only when faced with someone equally so." His tone softened, and he leaned in some, but did not venture past what was proper. "Please have the maid tend to your arm. It would mean a great deal to me if you would."

She exhaled, exasperated at his insistence. "I do not understand why."

"A part of me feels responsible. Whilst you did warn me, I did not believe your sister to be so determined. Most ladies would also loath ruining a gown. The colour of yours is so lovely with your complexion. It would be a shame to see it spoiled."

Her face burned at the compliment, but a glimpse of her sister's sneer over the earl's shoulder caused her eyes to widen. He peered back and despite the transformation of her sister's countenance to a sickly sweet expression, his jaw clenched.

With a resigned sigh, her shoulders dropped. "I will go. Please ensure you tell only my father and brother."

"I understand."

Without a backwards glance, she strode forward and through the double doors, shocked when a maid was already awaiting her on the other side.

"Lord Matlock indicated you were injured, miss. I was asked to tend to your arm."

The maid gestured to a chair, and she took a seat, the girl tutting when she saw the wounds. With a gentle touch, the maid pushed the pretty ruffles of her sleeves out of the way, and placed towels around to protect the fabric.

As she set to work, the earl entered and took a seat nearby. "I found your brother speaking with a Miss Abbot." He chuckled and leaned over to watch the maid as she worked. "He was quite put out that he had to abandon the lady to attend your mother and sister when they attempted to follow you from the room. I offered to ensure you were well, so he could request your father deal with your mother. He had no issues with my acting in his stead until he could come."

"I do not believe all of this is necessary. Once the bleeding stopped, I could have continued on as I was."

The maid tending her wounds pressed a cloth to one of the cuts that stung, and a hiss escaped her lips. "If you will pardon me saying, miss, but I have heard instances of similar injuries festering."

"You have?"

She gave a sly grin. "You should spend a season in Town. Some of the ladies there inflict such abuse on one another from time to time."

With a lift of her eyebrows, she shook her head. "I do believe our small neighbourhood suits me well, then."

"You would do well in London."

Rebecca turned towards the earl, incredulous at his assertion. "London sounds beyond my expertise. I much prefer a simpler life."

His gaze was earnest. "It does not have to be so complicated."

The maid placed a new cloth to her arm that stung as much as the first, and she winced. "May I ask how you are acquainted with Lord and Lady Sudbury?" Hopefully, he would take her cue to change the subject.

"Lady Sudbury is my sister. She invited me to spend a month complete at Warrington before my return to Matlock, and as we have always been close, I decided to accept her generous offer. Lord Sudbury's brother then determined he should be invited as well."

"And it became a house party."

"Yes, though I have enjoyed the sport."

The maid dabbed at her arm. "Miss, the bleeding has stopped, but I believe the injury should be wrapped to protect the silk of your gown."

She sighed in resignation at the ugly marks and nodded. "Very well."

"Your long ruffles should hide most of it, but Sophie will have a shawl to cover the bandage should you wish to return to the party."

The door behind the earl opened and Aubrey entered. "I apologise for not coming sooner. I made my excuses as soon as I was able." He started when her arm came into his view. "Sarah did this?"

She gave a slight shrug. "She was angry with me."

"For a matter beyond your control," he fumed. "Papa will not be pleased. I do wish you would allow me to introduce you..."

"It is of no matter, Aubrey." She pled with her eyes for him to leave both the situation and the discussion alone for the time being. "Lady Sudbury was kind enough to keep me close until the men returned from their drink and cigars. *I* made the mistake of thinking Sarah would not dare attempt something with so many people about, and left the countess' protection. I should not have done so."

With a look at the width of the cloth the maid was using to wrap the injured arm, Aubrey leaned in closer to her. "Questions will be asked if you return to the party bandaged. I will fetch our father, and we will make our excuses."

The maid tied off the bandage, and Rebecca leaned back into the comfortable chair. "Our early departure will make matters worse with Mother, and people may still talk."

"If you will pardon my intrusion," interjected the earl. "I can send a note in to Sophie. She can claim Miss Rebecca took ill and was given a room to recuperate. In the meantime, Miss Rebecca can remain within the library and read until you are ready to depart."

Aubrey stood firm and proud. "We could not accept such a generous gesture. I also hesitate to make such an imposition on our hosts. Sarah should not have conducted herself in such a manner."

The earl rose, so he was eye level with her brother. "Sophie will understand and would offer were she present."

"What would I offer, Brother?"

Their heads whipped in the direction of the doors where Lady Sudbury now stood. She moved with grace to the maid, who was tidying the mess, and stayed her actions with a hand to her wrist. "What has happened here?"

The countess' genuine concern did her credit, but the earl's suggestion to be secluded from the party was not necessary was it?

"It is merely an injury of no consequence, and I would prefer not to call it to the attention of your guests." She turned to Aubrey. "I left a shawl in the carriage. If you will but fetch it, it will not be necessary to intrude so on her ladyship's hospitality."

"Nonsense!" cried Lady Sudbury. "If you wish to return to the party, I have an ivory shawl that would be lovely with that colour green. It was a gift from Gerald, and I am certain he would not mind me loaning it to you."

The earl gave a small bow. "Indeed I do not. I hope you do not object, but I also suggested that if Miss Rebecca wished, she could remain in the library for the duration of the party. She would be unlikely to receive another injury, and would not attract attention to the present situation of her arm. If her absence is noted, you could claim she was indisposed and offered a room until her family took their leave."

"I do not mind your proposal in the slightest. In fact, if you wish to rest, Miss Rebecca, I always have a room or two prepared for parties. You never know when someone will take ill."

Rebecca was taken aback by their kindness. "I do not wish to impose."

"None of the suggestions are an imposition, my dear. You merely need to decide what you desire." Lady Sudbury took a seat beside her and placed a hand upon her forearm. "Unfortunately, guests are not always comfortable with one another and alternate arrangements must be made. I am certain my seating plan for dinner is where some of the responsibility lies, and I insist upon being a part of the solution."

Her brother stepped forward and gained the countess' attention. "You take too much upon yourself, Lady Sudbury."

"In this case, I am certain I do not." The lady gave a squeeze to Rebecca's wrist. "Have you made a decision?"

With a nod, Rebecca scanned the faces of all attending her before her eyes set upon the countess. "I believe I should like to avoid Sarah and my mother for the remainder of the evening. If it is all the same to you, ma'am, I prefer the library to a room. It seems less of a bother."

"Jane? Do you mind sitting with Miss Rebecca for the evening?"

The maid stood. "No, my lady. I will return these supplies to the housekeeper and return straight away."

"Then it is settled." Lady Sudbury grinned at her brother, who all of a sudden appeared ill at ease. "Will you be entertaining the lady, or shall I expect your return in a few minutes?"

He gave an abrupt tug to the bottom of his coat. "I thought to stay and keep the lady company. We would not want her to be bored."

The countess smirked. "Of course not. I will make your excuses. Perhaps, you had some sudden business from Matlock to address."

"An admirable story. I thank you."

She grasped her brother's arm and squeezed before she departed the room. Meanwhile, Aubrey peered between the earl and herself without making any move to return to the others.

"Go woo Miss Abbot."

His eyes set upon her and widened. "You should not..."

Rebecca laughed. "I should not make assumptions? I know of what I speak. My reputation will be protected by the maid's presence and Lady Sudbury's story. I know you wish to spend more time with Miss Abbot."

"Rebecca..."

"Go, Aubrey. I will be well."

He did not move, but stared with an open mouth, resembling a fish out of water, for a moment before shaking his head adamantly. "I am unsure if this is your best idea. If you were to rest in the room Lady Sudbury offered, I would feel more at ease about your not returning to the party."

"I mean to keep your sister company," stated the earl in a direct manner. "Nothing more. If she finds my conversation tedious or trite, she can banish me to the withdrawing room with the rest of the guests. I am at her mercy."

A giggle erupted, breaking the seriousness of the moment and drawing the gentlemen's stares. "I apologise, but there are few who would agree to be at my mercy."

His lip quirked on one side. "You do not frighten me."

"Perhaps I should," Rebecca quipped as the countess' maid returned to the room. Without comment, the young woman sat in a chair in one corner.

Aubrey's eyebrows advanced to his hairline as he watched their banter. "The pair of you got on well at dinner then. I had not noticed, but it is no wonder Sarah is furious."

"No doubt. You were observing Miss Abbot."

Her brother's face reddened. "Very well, I will return to the party. Please send word if you require anything or would prefer to depart."

With numerous backwards glances, Aubrey left through the same doors as the countess before him. Once the latch had clicked behind him, her gaze met the earl's. "I do not expect you to sit with me either. I am not a child who requires a nursemaid."

Despite her words, he appeared more amused than affronted. "I would not have stayed if I believed that of you."

"Why have you offered to remain? We did have some amiable conversation during the meal, but for most of our acquaintance, I have been less than civil in my address. I do not understand why you would want to keep me company."

He sat tall as he appraised her, searching her eyes. Rather than show reservation or intimidation, she did not retreat in the slightest, but held his steady look until he relaxed and leaned back into his chair.

"Very well. If I am to explain this, I will need to tell you a portion of my history, if you do not mind a bit of a tale."

She folded her hands in her lap. "I do not object. I have naught to do at the moment."

He chuckled. "You do enjoy being saucy."

"I hope you are not offended by my manner, sir." She could not help the small smile that crossed her lips.

"No, I find it refreshing."

His answer was unexpected, but for some reason, it pleased her.

"Are you aware that I was once married?"

Her pleasure faded with the turn in the subject matter. "My brother mentioned you were widowed. My condolences on your loss."

He took a deep breath and exhaled as if tired. "Thank you. Although, I must confess the marriage was not a happy one. My family chose her, and I adhered to their wishes."

Rebecca listened without interrupting, thankful her father would never go so far as to choose a husband for her! What a dreadful prospect!

"Charlotte was pleasant whilst we were betrothed. She feigned happiness and was diverting company prior to our marriage because she was in the presence of her mother or father. Once we were wed, however, she revealed her true nature. I have never met a person so angry or who could hold a grudge as she could.

"Within a year of our marriage, we had a daughter, Catherine. She was our only child. We put on a contented front for social gatherings, but we, for all intents and purposes, led separate lives within the same household. Almost two years ago, she began to have severe pains in her stomach, which progressed to a fever. Within a fortnight, she died."

Her heart ached for the unhappy years he must have spent tied to such a woman, yet it did not explain why he appeared to prefer her companionship.

"Whilst I was still in mourning, I realised I was considered an eligible bachelor once again when the young ladies and their mothers began courting my good opinion. Unfortunately, the similarities between their discourse and Charlotte's behaviour prior to our marriage were too marked for my comfort."

He shifted and cleared his throat, as if she had requested he bare his soul. "You ask why I seek your company?"

She nodded.

"Since I first stumbled upon you this morning, you have been honest to a fault. I annoyed you by confessing that I had spied upon you, and you had no qualms about upbraiding me for intruding on your privacy. I admit to being amused by your sharp tongue, but the quality I have appreciated most is your candour."

His explanation made sense, and she could appreciate his reasoning however sad it was. How long had he been so unhappy?

"Was your marriage of some duration?"

"My parents arranged the marriage with the intention of the wedding occurring soon after I left Cambridge. We were wed for eight years."

A small gasp escaped before she could prevent it. "You must have been young!"

"I was two and twenty. She was eighteen."

She took his measure as he sat before her. His green eyes watched her with honesty in their depths, and his tousled, sandy, brown hair appeared more dishevelled than earlier with a handful of strands escaping the ribbon. He appeared so old at that moment, and the dimple he had shown on several occasions was absent without any inducement to peek from its hiding place.

He mentioned a daughter. She must be near seven or eight since she was born so early in their union.

"Does your daughter favour you?" she asked, hoping to lighten the mood.

He gave a weak smile. "She takes after her mother."

His tone gave the impression that his daughter's resemblance to her mother was not in a good fashion, and she pressed her lips together hard. Could she have asked a worse question?

She took in his bleak countenance and smirked. "Do you often spy on young ladies as they dance in the fields?"

His eyes darted back to her face, but gave a hint of a twinkle. "Whenever I can. It is a favourite diversion of mine."

She gasped in mock affront. "Rake!"

A low, resonant laugh rumbled around the room and she bit her lip with a grin. He had been entirely too solemn, and it warmed her heart to see him smile again.

"Thank you."

What reason could he have to thank her? She was making amends for her poor choice of words.

"You owe me no thanks. I should not have asked such an intrusive question."

His brow furrowed. "Your question was reasonable, and most parents would be pleased to boast of their child. I see no reason for you to regret your words."

"They brought you sadness," she responded from her heart.

His countenance warmed. "Your sensitivity and kindness do you credit."

"Perhaps I am in a congenial mood this evening. I may be a petulant girl who stomps her feet and complains at the slightest provocation."

His head turned to the side, so he peered at an angle, with a slight grin. "I have seen your worst, and it is not as you describe."

She rolled her eyes. "After one day's acquaintance, you cannot claim to know me so well."

"On the contrary, Miss Rebecca. I believe I have sketched your character quite well, and I dare you to prove me wrong."

Chapter 6

When Rebecca set out the next morning, the ground was not as damp as during her previous walk. She had slept later than was her wont that morning due to the family's late return from the party the previous evening.

Her mother and Sarah had not dared to confront Rebecca before her father and brother, but she gave them no time to speak whence they returned, hastening up the stairs to her bedchamber as she ignored her mother's calls. Upon reaching her rooms, she had locked the door.

As she continued, trailing her hands along the trunks of the trees, she scolded herself for avoiding her mother. Father would not permit her mother to abuse her as Sarah had at Warrington. She should not have allowed her mother's presence to intimidate her so.

With a wicked laugh, she began to run through the trail she had established long ago until the forest ended and became an open field of verdant green. Her hand grasped a low hanging limb, and she used it to swing around the corner—where she hit something solid with an *oomph*.

Two hands steadied her as she was propelled back, unaware of what, or rather with whom, she had collided. The low chuckle that kept her company the night prior reached her ears before his wide grin and dimple came into view.

"I admit I hoped to encounter you this morning, but I had not expected you to jump into my arms."

An indignant gasp drew a breath of cool, fresh air into her lungs. "I did *not* jump into your arms, sir!"

He executed a curt bow. "I must have been mistaken since I did not see how you made such a graceful turn around the base of that tree."

She pointed in the direction of the trail. "There is a small dip in the earth as the forest ends. I often use that low limb to swing my way down to the field."

How beetle-headed of her to be running in such an unladylike manner! With a start, she gave a quick curtsy, which no doubt appeared an afterthought.

"Ah, I see. The activity is, I am certain, an enjoyable one."

"I do not do so too often," she defended, "lest I kill the limb of the tree."

His eyes twinkled as he gave a nod. "Then you would be unable to partake of the activity at all."

"Precisely."

An awkward silence settled between them for a moment before she heard a neigh, and shifted to see his horse, tethered to a tree behind him.

"You indicated you hoped to encounter me?"

The earl startled and reached into his pocket, withdrawing what appeared to be a letter. "My sister requests your company at tea on the morrow, if you can attend. She enjoyed your company last night."

"I will check with my father, but I believe I have no previous engagements." She took the proffered note. "I will pen a response to Lady Sudbury before teatime today."

As she held the invitation in her hand, she eyed him with a tilt of her head. "Was this all you required?"

"Oh! I suppose." He glanced to his horse and then back to her. "Do you ride?"

Did she ride? "Yes, but at times, I prefer to walk."

"Walking can be very refreshing." He gave a small wince, and she bit back a laugh. "Would you mind if I accompanied you?"

"I suppose not." With a gesture towards his horse, she lifted one side of her lips. "But, will your horse not be bored with such an endeavour?"

"He had a good run on the way here, and I will give him his head for the return to the stable. He will have his exercise."

"You could allow him to follow us."

He appeared pleased at the suggestion, and after removing his reins from the tree branch, he motioned toward the field with his free arm. "I hope you have not had an unpleasant encounter with your mother as a result of last night."

Her eye on the path, she gave a slight shake of her head. "No, but I departed this morning before she or Sarah left their bedchambers. I doubt I will escape her censure today, though my father promises he will not allow her to abuse me."

"You deserve no rebuke for your behaviour at the party," he defended. "On the contrary, you conducted yourself with more decorum than either your sister or your mother.

Out of the corner of his eye, he peered in her direction. "I am afraid I told Sophie of our meeting yesterday, and she placed you beside me at dinner for that reason."

Rebecca halted and her head whipped the remainder of the way around to face him. "You told her of my falling?"

"No, but I did indicate you had a mishap, and I escorted you home." His horse nudged his arm, distracting him for but a moment. "I hope I have not embarrassed you by confiding in my sister. We have always been close, and she was quite curious about my happy mood when I returned from my ride."

Her cheeks warmed as she searched for something in the distance at which to stare. "I am not embarrassed by your explanation. I just would not want my brother or father to hear that I had been sliding around in the muck."

His chuckle caused a sensation like butterflies taking flight within her stomach. "Then, it is not a common practice for you."

One pointed glance in his direction, and his laugh echoed across the hillside. "I suspected as much."

"I do not always find myself in the mud," she exclaimed as she began to walk once more, "but I have a bad habit of catching my skirt on a passing limb or falling. I might ruin one gown a year."

"That is not *so* bad. I believe Sophie ruined two or three one summer."

Her indignation calmed with his statement and his good humour. "She enjoyed the outdoors?"

"She still does, but she is more careful. Lord Sudbury also accompanies her most days on a ride or a walk around the park."

"He does?"

"Sudbury and I were friends prior to his courtship of my sister. I was inordinately pleased when he requested her hand in marriage. I knew she would be happy, and he would treat her as she deserved."

A smile could not help but grace her face at his care for his sister. "You are a good brother. I imagine Aubrey would be much the same."

"If I am not mistaken, he attempted to gain your agreement to be introduced to some of his friends last night in the library."

She frowned and quickened her pace. "I do not require his aid. It is not as if I am a spinster without family to care for me."

"Miss Rebecca!" The sound of his footsteps became louder just before he grabbed her by the elbow. "I apologise if I presume too much. As a brother, I know Fairchild wishes to do what is best for you.

"He cannot ignore that you came to harm at your sister's hand. If he were, then he is not the man I thought him to be."

She whirled around and glared as he released her with haste. "My brother is amongst the best of men. If he and my father do not act against Sarah or my mother, it is out of concern for my reputation and my future."

"Does your mother treat you with the same lack of respect shown by your sister?" His voice had dropped and his eyes searched hers, making it hard to hold his stare.

"My sister has long been my mother's favourite. She has compared Sarah many times to herself."

"But what of you and your brother?"

"She never doted on my brother, but she treated him well until he was old enough to censure her for her treatment of me. Since then, she courts his good favour—I believe because she fears her future should my father die—but Aubrey does not abide her false manner."

A strange garbled sound escaped her throat, and she swallowed hard. She would not cry!

"Sarah was the eldest, and whilst my father has never said as much, I am certain my mother hoped she would have no further children after Aubrey until I happened along. My father knew when I was born that my mother would not do her part in my upbringing, so I had a nurse and a governess. He taught me to ride, and he assisted the governess with my education."

The earl's head tilted to catch her attention. "Not many fathers would do as much. He is a good man."

"He is. I know few who are better."

"I hope you do not find me intrusive by asking, but has he attempted to correct your elder sister's behaviour?"

"He has, but my mother encourages her. Sarah seeks our mother's approval, not our father's. His rebukes fall upon deaf ears."

His forehead creased, and he stared at the ground as he mumbled, "Your brother wishes to see you married and away from both your mother and your sister."

"Yes, but..." Why was he so contemplative?

"I would be pleased to have you as my bride," he stated as though it were common for a stranger to propose marriage.

Her jaw dropped and her entire body began to shake. "You are mad!" She pivoted in the direction of the house.

With a frown, he stepped in her path. "I disagree. I have avoided the women of my acquaintance because they are scheming and manipulative, and I have no wish to enter into a marriage like my last. We may not have known one another for long, but you are honest to a fault, intelligent, and beautiful. You do not allow your mother or your sister to bring you melancholy—at least, not for any length of time."

"To what do these recitations lend themselves? To your illustration of my character?"

"No!" He took her hand, and she stared as his gloved hands enveloped hers.

Why did it feel as though her hand were bare?

"They are the reasons I admire you as I do. *They* are why I have sought your company since our first meeting."

She snatched her hand back. The sensations he was creating were not conducive to clear and rational thought. "Which was four and twenty hours ago! We are but strangers, sir. You must admit that such a hasty betrothal and marriage would not bode well for our marital felicity."

He was not too close in an improper way, but his nearness was unnerving. She took a step back, and the uncomfortable sensation he evoked was relieved. Regardless, she needed to away from him! It was impossible to think or make sense of his arguments when he continued to provide more to consider!

"Miss Rebecca, you must promise to think upon my offer."

She shook her head adamantly. "No!"

"No?"

"No, sir." She covered her face with her hands and took a deep breath in an attempt to gain her composure. "We are strangers, and I have never contemplated spending my life with a man I do not know. You also have a limited knowledge of me."

She lifted her head and gestured in the direction of Warrington. "You do not know if you could trust me with your daughter. If we were to marry, I would be as a mother to her."

"You would be a wonderful influence on Catherine." He was in earnest. It was displayed in an open fashion upon his features, but she could not accept him. He had to have no idea what he was about. "My daughter was indulged too much by her mother, as your sister is with her mother. She requires a steady hand, which I do not doubt you could possess."

A shrill laugh escaped her lips, and she clamped her hand over her mouth and shut her eyes tight. "I must go." With quick strides, she hurried away.

His heavy footfalls sounded from behind. "Miss Rebecca!"

She did not turn—she could not. Instead, she hastened down the path for home, not slowing until she stepped foot through the rear door near her father's study.

The door slammed behind her, rattling the windows in their frames, and she let out a heavy exhale, as if she had been holding her breath for the entirety of the walk through the woods.

As she made her way down the corridor and past the door to her father's study, he lifted his head from his work. "Rebecca?"

Chapter 7

At the sound of her father calling her name, Rebecca attempted a poor excuse for a smile, prompting him to set down his pen and lean back in his well-worn chair. "Come inside and close the door, dear."

When she was seated across from him, he took a moment to examine her, but she avoided his observation by staring out of the nearest window.

"What has made you return with such haste?"

"I happened upon an acquaintance and the meeting was upsetting." His eyebrows raised, but despite his obvious curiosity, she did not wish to speak of it. "Please do not ask me to explain."

"You are well, though."

Was she well? She just received a rather unromantic proposal of marriage that shook her to her very bones. No, she was not well!

"I merely require some time."

"You are certain?"

Without a knock or warning, Aubrey entered and relaxed when he noticed Rebecca. "There you are. I met Lord Matlock upon my return from the stables. He indicated you were upset when the two of you parted ways, and had trailed behind to ensure you made your way home without harm."

She covered her face and groaned. "What did he tell you?" Her hands muffled her voice, but it was no matter. Aubrey would take great delight in teasing her if he discovered the truth of the situation. "Did he think he could force me into marriage by informing you of our happening upon one another?"

She drew her legs up, rested her forehead upon her knees, and wrapped her arms around her legs. Why was she shaking again? What was it about Lord Matlock that had the ability to discompose her so?

"He said naught of marriage, Bec," he soothed. "Merely that you were overwrought, and he was concerned."

Realising she had exposed her own secret, she groaned.

"Lord Matlock offered for you?" Her father's voice held a note of wonder as Aubrey sat upon the edge of the desk, both men staring with incredulity in her direction.

Aubrey's surprised countenance broke when he gave a loud bark of laughter and slapped his knee. "I thought he seemed rather solicitous of you last night, and even Lady Sudbury requested your company." He looked to his father. "It is no wonder Mother and Sarah were livid. They must have recognised his partiality."

"It was no proposal of instant admiration. Besides, I refused his offer."

Her brother's eyebrows furrowed with a frown. "If he was not taken with you, then what other reason could he have for such a gesture—especially on such a short acquaintance? Whilst you do have a small dowry, it is not one an earl would be accustomed to receiving. We also do not boast of any grand connections, so it is not as though he is seeking an advantageous alliance."

"He wished to help me escape Sarah and my mother." The words stung and had a bitter taste.

A chuckle prompted her to stare at her father. "Why do you laugh?"

He made his way around the desk and knelt before her. "Sweetling, a man does not propose marriage to save a woman if he is indifferent."

"I beg to differ, Papa. If Sarah were to entrap one of the gentleman she chases..."

"I do not speak of women ensnaring men of means. If a man compromises a woman and then remedies the situation with marriage, he does so because he has some sort of feelings—though not always proper—for the lady in question, else he would not have compromised her."

His piercing look over his spectacles asked if she understood, so she gave a nod of her head.

"If a man proposes to save a woman, whether from a poor family or an unfavourable situation, he has an affection for her. He would not make the offer otherwise. He could just as easily offer her a much less respectable position."

"So you are implying the earl feels more for me than he would a mere acquaintance?" His theory was not plausible! The earl could not be so devoted after what—a day?

Her father gave a shrug. "It is probable. Though, it does seem quick for a simple evening spent in company..."

She squirmed in her seat, and her father's head gave an abrupt jerk back. "Were you acquainted prior to the dinner last night?" Aubrey's eyes were wide as horse chestnuts as he leaned closer.

"He may have found me walking near the west fields yesterday."

"Rebecca!"

Why was Aubrey so shocked? She had done nothing wrong!

"Why that tone? The meeting was innocent! I slipped on a patch of mud, so he helped me to stand. I took a bit of a chill from my damp dress; he gave me a sip of brandy, and then, afraid I drank more than I had, insisted I ride his horse home."

Her father was puzzled. "But you brought no strange horse to the stables yesterday."

"No, he placed me atop and led me to the edge of the back garden." With an abrupt motion, she planted her feet back upon the floor, swung her arm towards the window, and pointed. "I insisted I was well, that I did not require his aid. He would not listen!"

Aubrey began to chuckle. "What on earth were you doing when you slipped? Or was it something you said or did after the incident?"

Her face heated and her brother only laughed harder. "I would wager you do not want us to know, else you would have told us by now."

A level stare from her father made her gulp. "I was anticipating our evening at Warrington and the upcoming ball by dancing."

"You were dancing," he clarified.

"Yes, sir. I went to turn, and slipped on some mud—just as I told you. I heard him laugh, and when I was back upon my feet, I scolded him for spying."

Her brother's snort attracted her father's gaze. "Perhaps you should leave."

"What have I done?"

"This is not the time or the place to tease your sister."

A small part of her celebrated at her father's set down, and for a bit of fun, stuck out her tongue at her elder brother.

"You expect that to attract an earl?" Aubrey gestured towards her as her father turned.

"That is enough. You are not five years of age, Rebecca. You are one and twenty. Behave as such, please."

Her brother moved to sit in the chair beside her. "Do you think the earl will accept her refusal?"

Papa rose and seated himself along the edge of his desk, but made her uncomfortable by continuing to assess her. "I believe it will depend on several factors. If Lord Matlock proposed on a whim, he might be willing to wait until Rebecca feels more comfortable accepting, but if she insulted him with her refusal and wounded his pride, he may or may not renew his addresses."

"I did say he was mad," she said timidly.

Her father chuckled and Aubrey was aghast. "Please say you did not?"

"The offer took me by surprise! How was I to know he would propose marriage when we were discussing Sarah's tantrum?"

"Lord Matlock has been nothing but a gentleman in manner and address since I made his acquaintance. He did not have to sit with you after the incident, yet he did."

Her stomach clenched as she turned towards her brother. "I did not know what to say! He proposed marriage on a day's acquaintance! You must admit that you might say the same in my place."

"Not to an earl."

She rolled her eyes. "As if you would ever have to refuse an earl."

With a guffaw, her brother leaned back in his seat, a smug expression adorning his face. "No, I would not, thank goodness."

Her hands dropped to her lap; the note from Lady Sudbury crinkled in her pocket. Once she pulled it out and broke the seal, she read the invitation, smiling at the kind wording of the letter.

"Papa, Lady Sudbury has invited me to tea on the morrow. Do you think I could attend?"

He observed her with care. "When did this occur?

"Lord Matlock delivered the invitation this morning." Would Lady Sudbury still wish to spend time with her? "Would the invitation still stand?"

"I doubt Lord Matlock or Lady Sudbury are so fickle. I conversed with Lord Matlock after dinner and Lady Sudbury for a time before we departed. I found them both sensible and well-spoken."

"Will you attend?" asked Aubrey.

"I would like to get to know the countess. She was very kind when I spoke to her last night."

Her father gave a curt nod. "Then you shall go, but we will have to devise some excuse for your mother and Sarah, else they will insist upon joining you. I doubt they are invited."

With a glance at the missive, she confirmed his suspicions. "She indicates in the letter that she desires to know me better. No mention is made of my mother or Sarah."

He ran his thumb and forefinger along his jawline as he often did when he thought aloud. "If the weather is pleasant, would you mind riding? We could tell your mother you are visiting tenants. She will not seek you out, and you can depart from the servant's hallways to avoid her seeing your best habit."

"I do not mind."

Aubrey stood beside their father. "But, if the earl continues to pay court to Rebecca, our mother and Sarah will not stand by and idly watch her become the next countess."

She sighed and dropped into the back of the chair. "I do not want to worry about whether the earl will pursue me or not. I do not know if I want him to pursue me!"

With a clap of his hands, her father strode around and took his place at his desk. "I will pen a letter to your uncle. He once owned a small house in Bath, and offered me the use of it if we wished to holiday there. Perhaps, your mother and sister would enjoy the diversions of Bath for a time."

Another snort came from Aubrey. "She would have an entire town full of men to foist Sarah upon. Sounds a capital idea."

Her father finished a quick letter, sealed it, and handed it to her brother. "Please have this sent express. The sooner it arrives, the sooner we will receive a response."

When the door closed behind her brother, Papa levelled her with a steady gaze. "I once promised to tell you the history of myself and your mother. Do you still wish to hear the tale?"

A wary and unfamiliar sensation prompted her to sit straighter. Did she truly want to know? Her father's demeanour and reluctance to relate the story worried her.

He released a rough exhale. "You know very well that I have been reluctant to tell you. As much as your mother's neglect has injured you, I cannot regret it. You would not have become my dear girl had your mother influenced you as she has Sarah."

As her teeth dug into her bottom lip, she made her decision. "I want to know, Papa."

His fingers toyed with a paper upon the desk as he avoided her eyes. "I thought you might."

The man, who had always appeared so strong and capable, now held himself in a weary manner as he rose from the desk and moved to the window, where he stood with the appearance of looking, but not truly seeing what was beyond the pane of glass.

The clock on the mantel ticked, indicating the seconds passing, and Rebecca's fingers had just begun to tap along with the even sound when her father's voice began.

"I met your mother through your uncle, John, who was my good friend, as we attended Eton and later, Oxford together. He once visited this house during one of our breaks, and on more than one occasion, I stayed at his parents' estate for a month complete during the summer.

"Two years after we left Oxford, I received a disturbing letter from him, which detailed the ruin of his younger sister—your mother. She had made the mistake of trusting the son of a local landowner. The family was very wealthy but felt your mother was beneath them, so when she presented with child, the son denied the attachment as well as being the father."

"How terrible!"

Her father nodded. "Terrible indeed."

He sighed and began to pace back and forth before the fireplace. "My friend asked my advice on the predicament. His parents had prevailed upon your mother to be hidden away until the babe was born, yet she refused to be sent away. They were at a loss as to how to proceed.

"I remembered an amiable young lady from my visits. The girl I knew was pretty and shy, and I was appalled at this so-called gentleman and his treatment of her."

Rebecca closed her eyes in horror. "You offered to marry her."

"I did, and her brother accepted." He sat in the seat beside Rebecca and took her hand. "She was so sad and quiet when we were first wed. I tried to give her time to heal from the pain, but she remained so aloof towards me.

"Sarah was born five months after we married, and she devoted herself to being a mother. She doted on Sarah, and I saw no harm in it at the time. Two years later, Aubrey was born, and whilst she did not reject him outright, he was not treated with the same love and care his sister was."

A swift hand swiped away the tear that dampened her cheek. "You were Aubrey's father and not that other gentleman." Her poor father! He had sacrificed so much; his selflessness was never appreciated.

"Your mother claimed I had my heir and there would be no further children, yet you came along two years later. Your mother was displeased to be with child, and she never ceased to make me aware of that fact. Like Aubrey, you were sent out to live with one of the tenant families until you were weaned.

"When you returned, I hired a nurse for you and a governess for your brother. Your mother continued as always and my pleas for her to treat you as her own fell upon deaf ears."

"You never so much as said a word to indicate Sarah was not your daughter." How had he kept such a secret for so long?

"No, I always treated her as if she were my own. She was hardly at fault for her true father's abandonment."

"Did no one in the neighbourhood ever suspect?"

He gave a small bark of laughter. "As coincidence would have it, I had travelled to London on business a few months prior to marrying your mother. Most of the neighbours assumed we anticipated our vows."

Movement outside of the window drew her eye, and she could not help but smile at the sight of her brother whistling as he returned from the stable. "Is Aubrey aware you are not Sarah's..."

"I felt I *had* to inform him a few years ago. I had no wish to, but should I die, I did not want him to be taken unawares should your uncle or your mother broach the subject. I have reason to believe Sarah is as of yet unaware."

After turning away to hide the moisture in his eyes, he cleared his throat. "I never wished to tell you... I never wished..."

A wheezing breath was taken in and released as he fought for control. "Whilst your mother never took an active interest in you when you were young, she was never cruel to you or Aubrey. When you came out, the local gentry had all danced or called on Sarah and found her wanting. You may not have married yet, but you are favoured over her daughter, which she resents."

He covered his face with his hands and rubbed his eyes. When he removed them, he appeared even more tired, if such a thing were possible. "I should have found some way of removing her from Marysden before now, but I worried of the gossip." A ghost of a smile crossed his lips. "I also own no convenient estates in Scotland where she could be banished."

He shook his head. "You deserved better, and I am so sorry you never received it."

Her open arms enfolded him in an embrace. "I never lacked for your love. You did the best you could for all of us. It is not your fault my mother never valued the wonderful man she married."

"I can never regret your mother. If I had not married her, I would not have had you or your brother."

"Oh, Papa! If I could but see you happy." Her voice cracked as her father's shoulders shook. In her one and twenty years, she had never witnessed her father cry, yet he had lost his composure in her arms.

He pulled back and cradled her face in his palms. "My happiness is yours. If you believe you can find love with Lord Matlock, then do not let fear stand in your way.

"Regardless of what happens, I will find a way to protect you from your mother and Sarah. I swear to you I will."

Chapter 8

Escaping Marysden the following day had been easier than expected. Rebecca's mother and Sarah were to pay calls to a few women around the neighbourhood, which made her father's plan for her to ride her horse a stroke of brilliance. Her mother required the carriage for the day and would not be present to question her whereabouts.

How she anticipated the ride! The jaunt to Warrington would provide her time to think and make some order of her confusion in regards to Lord Matlock as well as the situation with her family.

Her father's revelations of the day prior had been unsettling, to say the least, and her father's reluctance to confide the long held secret was understandable. Not one to cry, after their talk, Rebecca had made her way to her chamber and released a legion of tears for all involved in the terrible situation: her mother for being a victim of the rake who ruined her, her father for becoming another victim through his marriage, and for herself as well as her brother and sister.

Today, however, was a new day, and the tears that flowed so freely the day prior were now over and spent. Her sympathy for her mother had not lasted long. Prudence Fairchild was no longer the innocent, unsuspecting girl who had been utterly deceived; rather, she had scorned the man who saved her whilst holding dear the sole piece of her ruin she retained. Her mother deserved no more of her pity.

The place where she first made the acquaintance of Lord Matlock caught her eye, and still mortified, she cued Beatrice back into a canter, determined to leave that less than graceful performance behind. She needed to become more poised and less impetuous, certainly less clumsy!

When she reached the front of Warrington, a groom intercepted her and held her mare as she dismounted. Once the butler ushered her inside and her outdoor garments were handed to a maid, she was shown to Lady Sudbury, who awaited her in a small drawing room to one corner of the house. It was a sweet little place with windows along two walls, giving it a light and airy feel.

"Miss Fairchild!" the countess exclaimed, rising from her seat. "I am so pleased you could accept my invitation."

The two ladies curtsied, and the countess gestured towards the sofa. Rebecca took one end whilst her host seated herself upon the other, but angled towards her.

Rebecca suppressed the urge to bite her lip. "I do apologise if my acceptance was late in coming yesterday. I am afraid we did not have a servant free until almost dinner."

Lady Sudbury gave a warm smile. "I am certain it is my fault for issuing such a last minute request. You see, my new brother and his wife informed us a few days ago of their wish to visit some friends today. It only occurred to me after the dinner party to invite you, so we might become better acquainted."

"I thank you for your invitation. My father and brother were to ride out and inspect the drainage on the north end of the estate. I would have been left to fend for myself, which is always a dangerous prospect, without your offer to join you for tea."

With a laugh, the countess examined her from head to toe whilst Rebecca attempted not to squirm under the scrutiny. "If you will pardon me for saying so, your manner and sense of humour are different than your mother and sister."

Rebecca made to retort, but the lady put up her hand. "Please do not take offense. We may not have spoken for long, but I could tell you were not of the same disposition.

She gave a slow shake of her head. "We are as different as chalk and cheese."

Their conversation was disrupted as several maids entered carrying the tea service as well as trays laden with teacakes and other delectable treats. They chatted about books and inconsequential matters until Rebecca placed her teacup on the table.

"I am relieved you did not find my blunt observation of your mother and sister objectionable, but after your sister's abominable behaviour at my party, I did not see much reason to beat around the bush."

"I do not mind your honesty, ma'am."

"Good," the countess exclaimed, catching Rebecca's undivided attention. "Then you will not mind me saying that the grin my brother wore after meeting you was the brightest I have seen in years."

Rebecca froze with her mouth open. How was she to respond to such a statement?

"I..."

An amused smirk adorned the countess' face upon Rebecca's stunned reaction. "Gerald has not noticed a lady in years, and I will have you know that he is a spectacular catch in London. Despite his marriage and the mourning period, women have not hesitated to set their caps at him."

A fire lit in Rebecca's belly. "I do not seek to catch anyone, ma'am, and I have no intention of setting my cap at a man either. I am unaware of Lord Matlock's feelings on the subject, but I daresay he would not appreciate such interference."

Lady Sudbury gave a tinkling laugh. "I do see why he likes you."

"Lady Sudbury..."

She gave a knowing smile. "Forgive me for baiting you, but most ladies would not care or would agree with what I stated. You take offense to my insinuating an attachment on either of your parts.

"Gerald indicated you were honest to a fault and quick to temper, and he is correct. Yet, I saw for myself how you disliked feeling a nuisance when you were injured. Our neighbours have spoken of you with the highest regard. The words generous, amiable, and charitable have been amongst their praises, which can also apply to Gerald. You and he would make a good match."

Rebecca did not wish to speak further of the earl. "You were kind to allow me to remain in the library."

The lady sighed. "I confess I felt responsible for what occurred. When Gerald mentioned his meeting you, I swapped the seating arrangement. Though I know naught of what happened that morning on the hill, I wanted to keep him in such good cheer, so I seated you beside him. I do apologise for the problems that may have precipitated."

With a sigh, Rebecca shifted in her seat. "I do not blame you for Sarah's actions. You could not know that she set her cap at your brother, or how she would react.

"But I do wonder at how you knew who I was? Lord Matlock and I never introduced ourselves to one another that morning."

The countess tapped her temple with a glint in her eye. "It was rather simple to deduce. Your mother and sister called upon me when I first came into the neighbourhood. Miss Fairchild does not have your ginger-blond hair, or hazel eyes.

"My brother was certain you were a gentleman's daughter and indicated he escorted you to Marysden, so I assumed you were the youngest Fairchild sister."

Rebecca set her hands primly in her lap. "How do you find our neighbourhood? Has everyone been welcoming?"

The lady did not answer but observed Rebecca with a smug smile. "You are changing the subject before I have discerned if you have an interest in my brother? I do think I should like to have you as a sister—if you are so inclined of course."

Her cheeks were aflame as she smoothed her skirt, avoiding the lady's eye. "At the risk of being rude, I have only just made the acquaintance of your brother, and I do not believe such a hasty judgement is in either my or Lord Matlock's best interest."

The countess took Rebecca's hand, giving it a small squeeze. "You will do, but I cannot have you calling me Lady Sudbury. Please call me Sophie."

After recovering from the shock of the lady's unexpected approval, Rebecca studied the woman across from her. Her expression was guileless and friendly. She would like to have her as a friend, even if she was being insufferable with her assumptions.

"Then you must call me Rebecca."

Sophie pivoted a bit further, but paused with a glance in the direction of the window. "I do not wish you to go, but I just noticed the sky appears as though the heavens will open at any moment. We should call your carriage and get you home before the rain begins to fall."

Her head whipped around to notice the dark clouds outside and groaned. She had been either enjoying the conversation or deflecting Sophie's comments and inquiries about Lord Matlock; she had missed the change in the weather.

"I am afraid I rode since my mother wished to call on her friends. We have only the one carriage."

The countess rose to pull the bell. "We shall send you in one of ours then and have your horse returned when the weather improves."

As Sophie returned to her seat, the sound of something hitting against the glass drew them to the window.

The countess gasped. "Hail! Well, you are stranded with us, now. I will not send you out in such foul conditions."

Rebecca winced as the pebbles of ice ricocheted off the window. "My father and brother will worry."

"Do not fret. We will attempt to send a servant when this clears."

Lord Sudbury entered with Lord Matlock not far behind. "I told you Sophie would not send Miss Fairchild back with how the sky appeared!"

"I never insinuated my sister lacked sense, Sudbury. I was merely concerned Miss Fairchild may have already departed, and her carriage might be caught in the weather."

"Well, she is safe and is to join us for dinner," Sophie informed him with a knowing look.

His gaze did not leave her as she averted her eyes unable to maintain the connection. "I am relieved to hear it."

"Rebecca," called the countess, "we should get you sorted for dinner. I think I may have a gown that will suit."

Rebecca followed behind until they reached Sophie's dressing room, scanning the countess' figure. It was doubtful Sophie had a gown to fit her since the countess was a good two inches taller.

When the door closed behind them, the countess moved to a trunk, opened the lid, and began to sort through what was inside. "Ah! Here we are!" One by one, two gowns were pulled from the middle of the bunch. Then, the countess led her to a bedchamber down the corridor where she laid the selections on the bed.

"These were gifts from Gerald. Before I was out, he would treat me to an occasional trip to the theatre, and I always received a new frock for the performance." Sophie ran her fingers through the frills at the base of the elbow-length sleeves. "I never had the heart to dispose of them or give them away. I was concerned they would be given to the ragman."

The fine silk and intricate embroidery was sure to be expensive, and Rebecca balked. "You hold these dear. I could not possibly…"

Sophie laid a hand upon her arm. "I do not see why not. I cannot wear them, and I am certain you will treat them well. I insist."

Since it would be rude to refuse when Sophie was so adamant, she acquiesced, and once her new friend showed her to a guest suite, she rang for a maid to assist her. Then, Sophie returned to her own rooms to change for dinner.

Dinner was an informal affair compared to the dinner party a few nights prior, although, the earl was also much more attentive. With Rebecca as the only guest, there were not as many people infringing on his ability to speak with her, and Sophie appeared content to allow him to steer their discourse.

When the men separated after the meal, the ladies adjourned to the music room so they could perform on the pianoforte when the men returned. As the two waited, the countess took the opportunity to play through her piece whilst Rebecca stood at the window and stared outside at the weather.

The rain, which had continued throughout the evening, had ceased, and though the park was sodden and wet she yearned to be out of doors. So as not to disturb the countess, she opened the door with care and slipped outside to the terrace where she walked to the edge to survey the gardens.

The steady sound of drips came from the trees and, with a graceful movement, she extended her hand to catch a few stray raindrops falling from the roof of the house. The smell of the air after a rain flooded her senses, and she took a deep breath, welcoming more of the lovely scent into her lungs.

She loved to be outdoors after a rain! A spring storm was her favourite, but she would not bemoan the fragrance of a September shower.

With a smile, she rubbed her hands together to dry the moisture, but jumped at the sound of a footstep behind her. A swift turn revealed the earl, wearing an amused expression and holding a glass in one hand and a cigar in the other.

"You enjoy the rain?"

She scanned the darkening park in appreciation. "I enjoy the scent of the rain, whether it before, during, or after a shower. Each has its own characteristic smell and can change depending upon the season, but I have always taken pleasure in sitting in an open window to read during such weather."

He took a step closer and appraised the gown lent to her by his sister. "Sophie's choice suits your complexion well."

An involuntary shiver spurred her to cross her arms in front of her chest, yet he caught her gaze and would not relinquish it as he stepped forward.

"Are you cold?"

He proffered his glass and she wrapped both hands around the bowl to bring the amber liquid to her lips. The sip did not cause her to cough and splutter as it had before, though it still burned its way down her chest to where it pooled within her belly. After one additional sip, she returned the glass, which he then brought to his lips.

She pointed to his cigar. "Is that enjoyable?"

His eyes left hers for a moment to assess the smoking tobacco in his hand then in a casual manner passed it to her. "Do not take a large pull. You do not want to be ill."

A sniff of the acrid smoke made her scrunch her nose, but she held it with care as she turned it and put her lips around the tip. One small draw brought the most putrid flavour she had ever tasted, and she gasped, drawing the smoke into her lungs.

Again, she was coughing and spluttering in his presence as he gave a low rumbling chuckle. "Perhaps not."

The cigar was removed from her fingers and his brandy pressed back into her palm. "Take a sip. I daresay it may soothe the sting of the smoke." The substantial sip made her gulp as her eyes burned and watered.

"Is that better?

With one last clearing of her throat, she bobbed her head. "Yes, thank you."

His voice caught her attention, and she was again arrested by his gaze. "It is just as well you do not care for the cigar."

Another step forward, and he leaned in so that his heated breath fanned against her neck. He did not lay a hand upon her or touch her in any manner, but he was impossibly close, his proximity caressing her though in actuality he did not. When had it become so warm? She could not breathe!

Her hair shifted as he inhaled, and her eyes fluttered closed. "And why is that?" Was that voice hers? Why was it so rough and weak?

"I much prefer the scent you wear to the smell of cigars. It is lavender, is it not?"

"Yes," she whispered.

"I would not like for you to smell of the men after dinner."

The low rumble of his voice was no longer at her ear, so she opened her eyes. His face was just before hers and was still impossibly close. She inhaled a shaky breath as he peered down to her lips.

Was it dark enough to hide her reaction to his presence as well as his words? How was she to respond to such a compliment? Should she thank...

"Miss Fairchild."

With a start, her attention jerked back to where he had shifted to a proper distance. Her heart was thrumming against her ribs at a frenetic pace and she could still feel the warmth of his breath against her skin. "Yes?"

"I have never thought to propose marriage to a lady on such short acquaintance, but it seems I have no restraint when it comes to you. You should return to the music room before I am tempted to breach propriety further than I have already."

Her eyes bulged. Whatever could he mean?

He glanced to her lips and back. "I do not wish to offend you any more than I did with the offer of my hand."

"Your proposal did not offend me."

He lifted an eyebrow.

"Despite my mother and my sister's dispositions, I am afraid to risk my future happiness with such a generous yet impulsive gesture. I do not wish a marriage as my parents endure."

"You are so certain that would be our fate?" He set his glass upon the stone ledge of the terrace to take her hand. His fingers held her with a delicate touch as if she were a fine piece of crystal. "Because I do not believe you resemble your mother in the slightest. You are kind and genuine."

A shaky laugh erupted from her lips. "I have hardly been kind. I argue with you more often than not. You would not desire to spend your life subjected to my whims."

Without removing his eyes from hers, he bent forward as he brought Rebecca's hand to his lips. She froze in her spot as a tingle radiated from his kiss and down to her shoulder, the fine hairs on her arms standing on end.

The sound of Sophie's last chord brought her back to the situation at hand, yet she did not want to relinquish the touch of his hand—or his lips. A voice screamed from within that she could not behave so. It was not proper! With an abrupt movement, she snatched her hand from his.

"I must return to your sister."

A swift pace brought her to the door of the terrace, where Sophie stood just inside. "There you are. Has the rain abated?"

The countess stepped outside and then back inside, closing the doors behind her. "There is a chill to the air."

Rebecca attempted to catch a glimpse of the terrace where she had stood with the earl, but he had disappeared. "I had not noticed."

"Would you care to practice before the gentlemen return?"

She gave a silent nod and moved to the pianoforte, but as she placed her fingers upon the keys, she silently cursed them to cease their slight trembling. She could not play when her hands were so uncooperative!

Despite the impediment, she began the étude by Handel and prayed she would not err too terribly; however, when she released the last note, she clenched and straightened her fingers. It was not their fault she had made so many mistakes, but the fault of what occurred with the earl. Soon, he would sit upon a chair in this room whilst she played. Could she manage with him present when he distracted her so well when absent?

She could not understand how, but she was aware of his presence before she turned to see him, and she stood from the pianoforte in order to allow Sophie to perform first. The earl, upon noticing her by the instrument, strode a direct path in her direction.

"Miss Fairchild, are you to grace us with a song?"

Sophie grinned and bit her lip as Rebecca attempted to demure. "I merely intend to play, but your sister should perform before me."

"Nonsense!" exclaimed Sophie. "You are my guest. I insist you take your turn at the pianoforte first."

"You will require someone to turn the pages." The earl stepped forward with haste to the instrument as his sister and brother stifled their chuckles.

As she took her place before the keys, she peered at the distinguished man beside her. "I do not require the sheet music. I know the piece from memory."

Her words did not deter him since he leaned not only forward, but also a little in her direction in order to reach the pages, a smug smile upon his lips. "Regardless, I will ensure the correct pages are before you in the event you have need of them."

"You are insufferable," she whispered.

He turned and spoke in low tones. "I merely wish to be close to you and this affords me an excuse within the bounds of propriety."

A slight snort escaped as she attempted to hold in a bark of laughter. "Yet you are decidedly not proper, sir."

"No one is without fault."

She clenched her hands together wringing them in an attempt to quell the nerves that had emerged again since the earl's entry. When she could give a false appearance of calm, she attempted to put her fingers to the keys, but they gave a quiver so she clasped her hands palm to palm.

"Take a deep breath." His resonant voice was soft and comforting. She exhaled as she placed her hands again to the instrument.

Despite her instruction, Rebecca kept her eyes down as she began to play in an attempt to forget he was not leaving her side, yet the task was nigh on impossible since she could hear the pages of the music turn. His mere presence was also tangible. How could she be aware of him without his touch?

Upon the completion of the piece, she grimaced. She had not performed poorly but had made two noticeable mistakes. Both errors had been due to Lord Matlock's shoulder brushing against hers.

If he had listened from a chair across the room, she would not have made the mistakes. She told him she had not required his help!

Sophie rose from the sofa. "That was lovely!" The countess then turned her attention to her brother. "I am impressed, Gerald. I was not aware you knew how to read music."

Rebecca's head whipped around in time to catch the earl turn as red as a beetroot. How diverting to see him as discomposed as he usually rendered her!

"That was ungenerous, Sophie." He did not sound angry, but his eyes darted to Rebecca. Was he concerned for her reaction?

With a sly tone, she raised an eyebrow at the countess. "Perhaps Lord Sudbury would care to turn the pages for you?"

Sophie's eyes darted to her with amusement. "I will welcome my husband should he desire to attempt it."

As Sophie and her husband took their places at the pianoforte, Rebecca sat upon the sofa with Lord Matlock on the opposite end. At an urge she could not explain, she peered in his direction.

When her friend's performance concluded, she praised Sophie's efforts, yet could not have described the performance if asked. She had been too distracted by the tall gentleman seated nearby.

Chapter 9

Despite the dismal weather of the day prior, the morning dawned with a brilliant blue sky and a scattering of clouds. The ground was moist, yet Rebecca did not mind the damp earth since she was simply pleased to be out of doors!

Her horse ordered, she waited as the groom saddled Beatrice and cinched up the girth.

"Sophie could not convince you to remain for the day?"

She swivelled about to find Lord Matlock dressed for a ride. "Sophie is kind to offer, but I should return home. I do not want to be an imposition."

"You could never be regarded as such. My sister takes great pleasure in your company."

A smile came unbidden to her lips. "I enjoy her company as well. She did invite me to tea again next week."

"I shall look forward to the occasion." His words were sincere as he gave a small bow.

"Miss," interrupted the voice of the groom. "Your horse is ready."

Beatrice nuzzled her arm, so Rebecca gave her a pat on the nose. "Would you hold her for a moment, please?"

The groom gave a nod as she lifted the saddle flap and began to adjust the girth.

The earl stepped beside her and placed a hand between the strap and the horse's chest. "Is that not too tight?"

"One would assume so, but if it is not tightened further, the saddle and I will slide down her side before we have ascended the hill."

She flattened the flap to find his eyebrows raised. "I had a friend at Cambridge whose horse was similar. Mine manages to loosen his girth some, but not to such an extent."

With a chuckle, she patted the horse's neck. "Beatrice has always been recalcitrant. Papa said she required someone as stubborn as she for a rider, which made me perfect—there are few people as intransigent as I."

He grinned. "I was going to ride to Marysden to call on your father. Would you mind if I accompanied you?"

With a bite to her lip, she gave him a quick appraisal. He did not seem up to mischief, but he did enjoy discomposing her. At present, however, his manner was open and earnest with no hint of mischievousness. "No, I would welcome the company."

The groom led her mare to the mounting block, she climbed atop, and walked Beatrice in circles for a few minutes until the earl's horse was saddled. Once he joined her, they started in the direction of her father's estate.

"Do you enjoy a good race, sir?" she asked with a smirk.

"Pardon?"

With a cluck, she took off towards the hill, the cool morning air whipping against her cheeks. The sound of steady hoof beats were advancing from behind, so she leaned forward in the saddle and gave Beatrice her head until they reached the first fence.

Beatrice cleared the hurdle with no difficulty and Rebecca peered over her shoulder. The earl's stallion was quite a bit larger and should have been outstripping her by now. Why was he holding his mount back?

She took the gentler slope, not surprised when he overtook her just as she reached the top. He slowed to a walk as she came alongside him.

"You ride well—very well, though I admit to almost closing my eyes when you took that fence." His praise prompted her to grin.

"I ride with Aubrey often, though he has never waited for me to open the gate to follow. I had to learn to jump or be left

71

behind." She tilted her head to get a better view of his face. "How long were you holding your horse back?"

"I caught up near the base of the hill," he admitted, "but I am unaware of the temperament of your mare. I feared she might bolt when we passed in an attempt to maintain our pace, so I reined Hermes in until we neared the top."

His confession riled her, so she cued Beatrice to a brisker walk. Lord Matlock did not lag behind for long and was soon once again beside her. "You are angry."

"I am a proficient rider. You need not coddle me."

With a swift hand, he leaned across, grasped her reins, and stopped her mount.

She turned with an abrupt pivot. "Unhand my horse, sir."

"Please do not take insult to my caution as I merely wished to ensure you were unharmed. You can be assured that I shall not underestimate you again."

His eyes begged her to understand, and she could not maintain her rigid posture, relaxing her stiff stance in response to his plea.

"Then I shall look forward to our next race." A wayward curl blew across her eyes, but the earl's fingers anticipated hers to remove it. The gentle brush of his glove across her brow caused a frisson within her belly, which made her uncomfortable, so she drew her horse away with a tug of the reins.

He made as though he would speak, but she urged her mare forward into the woods. His horse was not far behind based on the crunching of the fallen leaves upon the ground.

They rode in silence until they reached the stable at Marysden when Lord Matlock rode past to dismount before her. When the groom took her horse's reins, the earl was beside Beatrice with outstretched arms to help her to the ground.

She never relished the smarting pain in her feet when they came in contact with the hard earth during her dismount, so she begrudgingly allowed him to help, placing her hands upon his shoulders as he did so. His hands enveloped her waist, and she could not meet his eyes with equanimity, so instead, she stared at his cravat. With a hand to his offered arm, they headed in the direction of the house.

"Whilst I am capable of dismounting on my own, I thank you for your aid."

"Sophie does not ride often, but when she does, she does not enjoy dismounting. She claims it pains her feet. I thought to purchase a smaller horse, but she would not hear of it. Her current mount is well-suited for her. We were loath to trade him for another."

A bob of her head indicated her understanding. "I feel much the same of Beatrice."

As they rounded the corner, the front of Marysden came into view as Miss Abbot exited, and noticing their presence, walked in their direction. Rebecca released the earl's arm and strode past him to greet her.

"Emma!" she called. "I am sorry to have missed your call."

Emma smiled as she drew near. "From what your brother tells me, it could not be helped. Lady Sudbury was prudent to have you remain for the evening. The weather was truly dreadful."

Lord Matlock came to her side and gave a bow. "Miss Abbott, it is an agreeable day for a walk."

A slight curtsy accompanied a smirk from her friend. "Yes, it is, Lord Matlock."

With another quick bow, he glanced to Rebecca out of the corner of his eye. "I hoped to call on Mr. Fairchild this morning. If you will excuse me."

"Of course, please give my regards to Lady Sudbury."

He acknowledged Emma's statement with a nod and walked with a purposeful stride towards the house.

Her friend's eyes gave an amused twinkle. "He appears rather taken with you."

"I doubt he feels more than an infatuation. We have known one another but a few days."

Emma put a hand to her forearm. "My mother once confessed that she knew she would marry my father upon their first acquaintance." Her friend's worried tone drew her attention. "Rebecca, you love with a fierceness that is rare—all you do is for your father and your brother, yet, over the last few years, you have become more circumspect in who you allow near your heart. You do not even confide in me as you once did."

"I..."

"Lord Matlock is known here and in London as an exemplary gentleman. Do not allow your quick wit and sharp tongue to prevent an attachment between you."

Before Rebecca could respond, she caught a glimpse of Mrs. Mallory beckoning to her from the front door. She furrowed her brow, and Emma turned in the direction of the house.

"It seems your housekeeper has need of you." Emma gave a small squeeze to Rebecca's arm. "Please heed my words. I only desire your happiness."

After a quick embrace, Rebecca hastened to the front door where Mrs. Mallory waited. The housekeeper did not tarry, but jerked her within the house.

"My goodness! Whatever is the matter?" In her lifetime, Mrs. Mallory's present agitation was not a common occurrence.

"It is Miss Fairchild, miss. She insisted to Lucy that Lord Matlock was to be brought to a drawing room rather than your father's study."

She furrowed her brow. "Is Papa occupied at the moment? If that is the case, I do not believe he would make the earl wait."

"He requested your mother attend him not a quarter hour ago, but it is the look I witnessed in your sister's eye as she ascended the stairs just prior to my summoning you. She also insisted upon the parlour upstairs."

Rebecca's stomach dropped, and she took off through the hall to the servant's corridor. With her skirts hiked to her knees, she took the stairs in an unladylike fashion, pushed off the wall when she reached the first floor, and skidded to an abrupt halt at the servant's entry to the parlour.

They never showed guests to the family's drawing room, which was where she, her father, and her brother spent their evening after dinner, her mother often using the more newly decorated drawing room on the ground floor.

Sarah had to be making an attempt at a compromise. The drawing room on the ground floor was adjacent to her father's study. Had she used that room, someone would be more likely to happen upon the situation before Sarah could accomplish her goal.

Her gut roiling, Rebecca clenched her fists and released them. Sarah thought of few people beyond herself, but this was appalling! How could she?

In as silent a fashion as she could manage, Rebecca turned the latch and pulled the door, which blended into the oak panelling inside the room, towards her until a tiny opening allowed her to see within. The earl was standing nearby as Sarah watched him from near the entrance with a predatory gleam, dropping the key to the outer door down the bodice of her gown.

Chapter 10

"I would ask you to unlock and open the door, Miss Fairchild." His voice held a sterner tone than Rebecca had heard in the past.

"I think not," said her sister with a smirk. "I have no intention of allowing you to leave without our betrothal." His reaction was not discernible from where Rebecca stood, but she began to shake, seething at her sister's ploy.

"You avoided my mother and myself at Lady Sudbury's dinner, favouring my dowdy younger sister, but she knew she should not engage you. If she had left well enough alone, you might be calling on me instead."

He gave an adamant shake of his head. "I was well aware of your intentions that evening, I assure you. I disregarded you since you are not where my interests lie." His tone was furious, yet he kept it under regulation since his voice was not any louder than was his wont. "Regardless of your actions today, you shall not force my hand. I will not marry you."

Sarah grasped her bodice with both hands and rent it apart, splitting it down the left ties of the centre panel, turned towards the outer door, and began to pound. Lord Matlock had pivoted in an instant to face the wall.

With her sister preoccupied banging and bellowing at the top of her lungs for someone to come to her aid, Rebecca opened the servant's passage, reached inside to grasp the earl by his sleeve, and tugged him into the corridor, closing the door with haste. Any sound she made no longer mattered due to the uproar her sister had created.

Lord Matlock made to speak, but Rebecca put her finger to her lips as Mrs. Mallory's voice carried through the parlour.

"Miss Fairchild, what have you done to your gown?"

Rebecca bit her lip. Her sister's bewildered expression when she realised the earl was no longer there would certainly be a sight to see! Sarah had always forgotten the servant's doors since they appeared to be a normal part of the wall. That Sarah never used that room was another factor.

"Lord Matlock!" began Sarah in a breathless tone. "He was here!" Her voice changed to the screeching pitch with which Rebecca was more familiar. "The earl *was* here in this room!"

"Miss Fairchild, I know not of what you speak, but if I were you I would go and change your gown before your mother sees it or before Mr. Maddox happens upon you in such a state. Your mother would not be too keen on your marrying an aged butler."

The earl's low chuckle gave Rebecca reason to whirl around and cover his mouth with her hand. Sarah could not discover them within the servant's corridor or there would be hell to pay with her mother.

Her sister's characteristic foot stomp rattled the house followed by her heavy steps fading down the corridor until a door slammed, rattling the windows. Sarah had retreated to her bedchamber.

Lord Matlock removed her hand from his face, but did not relinquish his hold upon it. "How did you know?"

"Mrs. Mallory summoned me from outside when she suspected. I often use the servant's corridors to avoid Sarah and my mother, and I assumed she would forget about the door, which she did."

"I owe you a debt of gratitude that cannot be repaid—you and Mrs. Mallory."

She shook her head. "You owe me nothing. Although I do not think Mrs. Mallory would turn down some good tea or drinking chocolate if you wish to reward her in some fashion."

A devastating smile emerged as she spoke. That one dimple—the one she was so fond of—appeared from its hiding place. The earl lifted her hand to his lips and pressed a fervent kiss to the back.

Heat crept up her neck to her cheeks. A servant could happen upon them at any time, and she would be almost as compromised as Sarah would have been, had she succeeded. She pulled him towards the stairs, and he obediently followed as she headed in the direction of her father's study.

When they reached the entry, they paused at the sound of voices. Her father must not have concluded the discussion Mrs. Mallory had mentioned with her mother.

"I have no desire to travel to my brother's at present. Sarah will yet ensnare the earl if I have my way."

Her father scoffed. "The earl wants naught to do with either you or Sarah. He determined what the two of you were about at Lady Sudbury's party. He has managed, without rudeness, to avoid an introduction to the two of you by design. He will not offer for your daughter."

"And I suppose you expect him to offer for yours!" her mother spat. "She does not have the personality to make it within the Ton—or the looks. The earl would be an imbecile to choose such an ill-favoured little thing."

"May I remind you that you are insulting your own daughter as well?"

Her mother's response was not audible, but the earl's fingers tightened around her hand, garnering her attention. The alcove, where the servant's passage to the study was hidden, was narrow, so they had no choice but to remain close—too close.

The tips of his fingers traced her temple and down the contour of her cheek. "The first time I set eyes upon you, I thought I had never seen a lady so beautiful."

Her heartbeat was so fast, and it pounded so against her ribs. Was she out of breath as well? She attempted to speak, but the words would not come.

"Do not tell me I have rendered you speechless." The breath from his amused whispers warmed her cheek. Was he drawing closer?

His fingers brushed an errant curl from her temple as he bestowed a soft kiss near her hairline. Gooseflesh erupted down her neck and back as a small gasp escaped her throat.

His lips found her cheek, depositing another kiss, before he pulled a hairsbreadth away from her. His warm palm came to rest where her neck and shoulder joined. "You are lovely."

"Perhaps you are blind," she managed to quip. The light was dim, but she could still make out how his eyes bore into hers.

Her mouth was dry and her breathing shallow as he gradually leaned forward to capture her lips. She froze, uncertain of what to do, yet unable to push him away.

When he pulled back, his forehead met hers. "I am not blind. I have wanted to do that since your impassioned glare upbraided me after your fall into the mud."

"Beauty is in the eye of the beholder." Her voice sounded as though she were about to lose it. "You might believe me handsome, but you are alone in your estimation of my charms."

He shook with silent laughter. "Mine is not the only opinion. I assure you. I heard you mentioned as handsome prior to making your acquaintance."

"You had a preconceived notion of my looks prejudicing you, then?"

He drew back, about to retort, when she began to giggle softly. His lip quirked up with amusement. "You enjoy baiting me."

"I confess I do."

The voices within the study had become raised, and they both turned in the direction of the din.

"I will *not* travel to my brother's!"

A loud slam reverberated through the panelling. Her father must have struck his desk as he was known to do when angered. "It is settled, Prudence. I had hoped to send you and Sarah to Bath so not to impose upon your brother, but his Bath

79

home is let at the moment. Instead, you shall remain with him and his family for a month complete, and as you will be so close to Bath, perhaps he might be persuaded to accompany you thither for a sen'night or so."

"I shall never forgive you for this!"

"A heavy weight to bear, but I am certain I shall survive. You have forgiven me precious little in the past five and twenty years. I believe I can withstand your disapprobation this time as well. I shall receive another express from John directly with arrangements for your travel. If you do not instruct the servants to pack, I shall do so for you."

With a sigh, Rebecca dropped her head back against the wall. Poor father! He had paid a dear price for helping a friend and his sister. Would he never find peace?

Another door slam indicated her mother had departed the study, and Rebecca straightened. She made to open the passage, but the earl tugged her back by the hand he still held.

A small line appeared between his eyebrows. Why did he appear worried?

"Allow me to court you."

Her eyes widened, and he shifted to cradle her face in his hands.

"I know you fear how swift my feelings have arisen, but I assure you they are not as simple as infatuation. I want to know all of you—your loves, your likes, your dislikes. The more I am in your company, the more I find to appreciate of your wit and character."

She removed his hands, yet did not relinquish them. "I know nothing of society or London. You cannot desire a wife who would not fit in amongst your peers and their wives?"

He scoffed. "The ladies in Town are fickle. Even if you were born into that world, they may find reasons to spite you, yet you have a multitude of qualities that will make you a formidable countess. You boast of intelligence, amiability, and a generous heart, which are infinitely more important than a knowledge of the Ton." He looked down to their joined hands and entwined his fingers with hers. "I care not for what those of society believe. I care for you, and that feeling grows with every moment I am in your presence. Allow me to prove that I know what I am about. Allow me to prove to you that I am your future—that you are the lady I wish to wed."

Her vision blurred as tears welled in her eyes. How could he be so certain? This was so hasty, and her chest constricted with the anxiety of what it would mean if she agreed. But what if she said no? Could she bear to see him depart when the time came?

The fear of his being compromised by Sarah came to mind, and it gave her pause. She had fought against his advances, yet her heart was touched regardless of the short duration of their acquaintance. Were a mere few days enough to attach two people to one another?

His shoulders sagged at her reticence. "You need not say if your answer is no."

His forlorn expression tugged at something within her chest and pained her. "But I am in agreement," she blurted.

A transformation she had not anticipated occurred as he broke into a brilliant smile. "You are certain?"

The heaviness in her chest disappeared with his change of mood, and she gave a reluctant bob of her head. "I am."

He tugged her into his embrace, his hand resting upon her waist with a gentle touch. With a long breath, she inhaled deeply the subtle scent of cloves and cinnamon that permeated his coats, finding comfort and a sense of belonging in his arms. After a moment of indulgence, she placed her palm to his broad chest and pushed herself back.

"I cannot promise to be fearless. I..."

He allowed her to withdraw, trailing his fingertips along her neck to her arm as she stepped back. "You may be undaunted by many things, but I have noticed how you guard your heart. I do promise to protect it as assiduously as I do my own."

Before she could utter a word in response, the door opened to reveal her father, his jaw agape as he realised who was standing in the corridor.

"Since Marysden is not haunted, I knew someone would be behind the servant's entry, but I had not expected the two of you." His gaze ventured to where the earl's hand still supported her forearm and her palm rested on his. With a swift movement as though she were being stung, Rebecca tore her arm from his touch, her entire body burning in mortification.

Her father peered between them both for a moment until she could take it no longer. "We were hiding from Sarah and my mother."

His head tilted down, and he studied her over his spectacles. "Your mother just stormed from the room. Both of you are aware of her exit, are you not?"

"Yes, sir," agreed Lord Matlock. "I accompanied Miss Rebecca on her return from Warrington to speak with you, but the maid showed me to a first floor drawing room."

The furrowed brow her father wore spoke volumes as to his concern and confusion over the earl's tale. "That is a family room. Guests are always received on the ground floor."

"Sarah ordered him brought there. Mrs. Mallory informed me, and I used the servant's corridors to reach him before it was too late."

With a groan, her father closed his eyes. "Dare I ask what she attempted?"

"Sir," interrupted Lord Matlock, "this might be easier to take sitting down."

He gestured them inside his study with a nod and closed the door behind them. Rebecca sat in her usual chair before his desk whilst the earl took one beside her.

Once her father was seated, the earl cleared his throat, ill at ease with the conversation at hand. "As I said, I was shown to the first floor drawing room where I remained but a moment before Miss Fairchild joined me. She closed the door behind her, but when I objected, she laughed."

Her father covered his face with his hands. "Is that the extent of her actions?"

"I am afraid not."

With a glance between the two, Rebecca slid to the edge of her seat to garner her father's attention. "Upon reaching the servant's door, I discovered Sarah had forgotten to lock it, so I opened it just far enough to see the happenings inside." She glanced at the earl. "Lord Matlock was standing near the servant's entrance as Sarah told him how she wished to force him into marriage. When he refused, she ripped the bodice of her gown with both hands and began pounding upon the outer door."

"Please be assured that I turned away when I became aware of Miss Fairchild's intentions. I heard the fabric tear, but no more."

Her father leaned back in his chair, staring at the ceiling with a heavy exhale.

"Sir?" asked Lord Matlock.

Her father's hand ran through his hair as he drew himself up in his seat. "I must apologise for Sarah, my lord. I cannot but express my horror and disappointment at her actions, and I do swear that I shall reprimand her for her behaviour. She will not be in your company again."

The earl shook his head. "Miss Rebecca removed me from the presence of Miss Fairchild as your eldest turned to alert the household, and I confess I overheard enough of the earlier conversation with your wife to know that you do not condone Miss Fairchild's actions."

A weary sigh came from her father. "I would never force your hand with Sarah. A public airing of her schemes would likely harm Rebecca's reputation, but I hope you would not..."

"I have no reason to make public the circumstances of this morning." His tone was firm and sincere.

Rebecca made her way around the desk to kneel beside her father. "Are you well?"

He nodded, albeit reluctantly. "I shall be, my dear. Do not concern yourself with me."

She pressed her lips to his forehead. "I love you, Papa," she whispered near his ear.

Lord Matlock cleared his throat. "Sir? Whilst we are here, I desire to speak with you on another matter."

With a start, her father perked up. "You do?"

The earl nodded as he squirmed a bit. "I feel I should first explain my reticence in being introduced to your wife and eldest daughter. I have wished to apologise for any slight you might have perceived to yourself."

Her father began to wave his hand before him. "Please. I understand why you had no wish to be in company with my wife or Sarah. I do not fault you, and I never took offense." After a quick glance in her direction, he levelled a glare towards the earl. "First? Then am I to hope your other explanation pertains to the familiarity you and Rebecca displayed in the servant's corridor a moment ago?"

"Yes, sir." Lord Matlock stood and began to shift upon his feet. "Sir, I have requested the honour of a courtship with Miss Rebecca. She has accepted."

Her father's eyebrows rose as he turned to her in astonishment, yet before he could say a word, Aubrey burst into the room as though someone had set their hounds upon him.

"Papa!"

Chapter 11

1813

Elizabeth gave a weak grin. The pains were worsening, and they had yet to hear from the mid-wife. The stress of wondering why they had not received word of Mrs. Hewett added to her unease whilst she shifted and situated herself into a more comfortable position amongst the pillows.

The dowager brushed a few curls back from Elizabeth's face. "Are you certain you wish for me to continue?"

"I do!" She took the dowager's hand and gave it a squeeze. "I am enjoying the tale immensely. It is a welcome distraction from the process, and that Mrs. Hewett has yet to arrive.

With a shaky chuckle, she wiped a bit of moisture from her forehead with her free hand. "I must say I am quite astonished by the impulsivity shared by Fitzwilliam and your husband. I now understand why you were not more shocked by our hasty betrothal."

Grandmamma gave a small smile. "I could have objected, but I remember the feelings involved when Gerald pursued me so soon after our first acquaintance. He was so sure of himself, though I did not simplify matters.

"If I had voiced my concerns or objections when the two of you first arrived in London, Fitzwilliam might have absconded with you to Gretna Green. I needed to be certain the two of you were well-matched. I did not oppose your betrothal until my grandson began behaving in such a beetle-headed manner.

The next pain bore down upon her and Elizabeth gripped the bedclothes, digging her fingernails into the tender flesh of her palm. "When you threatened to take me to Ireland?" she grit out.

"Yes." The elder lady moved behind her and began to rub her lower back, prompting a groan. "With Gerald, we both recognised the attraction for one another, though I had a more difficult time yielding my heart, despite every fibre of my being telling me to give myself over to him."

"You should tell this story to Fitzwilliam. He might take pleasure in the knowledge that he shares such an impulsive nature with his grandfather."

A blushing Grandmamma leaned forward and placed a hand upon Elizabeth's belly as the pain subsided. "I will leave this for you to tell him."

"I do not believe I could do it justice."

"I would have to disagree," came Fitzwilliam's low voice.

She started and turned in his direction. "Fitzwilliam! I did not think you would return until Grandmamma sent for you."

He strode forward and seated himself upon the side of the bed. "I meant to visit with father, but I could not bring myself to go further than our sitting room. I have been sitting upon the floor by the door listening to Grandmamma's story."

Grandmamma smirked at her grandson as she moved to a nearby chair. "You managed to remain with your cousins for Thomas's birth."

"I found it exceedingly difficult to be so distant, even after Elizabeth tried to strangle me by my cravat."

Elizabeth chuckled. "I did beg your forgiveness for that offense."

"That you did, my dear, but I thought since Mrs. Hewett is not yet present I might join you until I am shooed from your chambers."

"I am uncertain if Mrs. Hewett would force your exit," teased Elizabeth. "The nature of her smiles and blushes when you spoke to her a se'nnight ago were indicative of a woman who is taken with you."

Her husband's jaw dropped. "Should my mother have lived, Mrs. Hewett would be of a similar age!"

Grandmamma smirked. "She did titter as Mrs. Reynolds escorted her from the room and confided that she had seen few so handsome."

He narrowed his eyes and studied them both. "You are teasing me! I knew you could not be serious!"

Elizabeth bit her lip to keep from giggling. Fitzwilliam was always so swift to believe they were having a laugh at his expense. Women often reacted in such a way when he spoke to them, yet he never noticed or remarked upon the behaviour.

"I should know not to trust such outlandish tales from the two of you." He stood, removed his topcoat and cravat, and took a place with his back against the headboard, helping to situate Elizabeth so she rested against his chest.

Grandmamma did not avert her eyes at such familiarity in her presence. "Do not mind me."

Fitzwilliam's chest shook with laughter, but Elizabeth closed her eyes and rested her head against him. With a deep breath of his familiar scent, she was more at ease.

"To return to the story of you and Grandfather," he remarked. "If you remember, I once asked if he had ever introduced you to cigars, and with a clever retort, you avoided confiding the truth."

The dowager, who was rarely flustered, reddened and shifted. "I suppose I should not be embarrassed to relate such personal details when I so often see the evidence of affection in your marriage, yet I am not describing your emotions or actions, I am relating my own. I am more reticent with my most personal memories."

"Grandfather accepted and adored you for who you are, Grandmamma. Elizabeth and I have often discussed how under your powdered wig and stomacher1, you were not the typical daughter of a gentleman."

The elder lady pointed a finger in her grandson's direction. "I *never* wore a wig! I admit to being required to wear hairpieces, so my maid could style my hair in the latest fashion. I powdered my hair. But, I could not abide the wigs!"

Elizabeth tensed as another pain overwhelmed her. In an attempt to regulate her breathing and to forget the terrible tightening of her protesting muscles, she focussed even more on the voices of her husband and the dowager.

"You never wore a wig?" Her husband's deep voice rumbled. "Elizabeth and I have seen portraits of you and grandfather, the likenesses taken soon after your wedding. Your hair…"

"Was large, as the style dictated, but was mostly my own. Your grandfather wore wigs on occasion when it was required by social engagements or the House of Lords, but we both found them hot, scratchy, and unpleasant."

Out of breath, Elizabeth gave a weak laugh. "Whilst I am enjoying the conversation, I requested a story which is being sorely neglected."

A kiss was deposited into her hair by her husband, and despite her uncharacteristic complaining, she peered up to find him wearing a smile.

"My wife will not be satisfied until you tell us all."

"Oh dear," remarked Grandmamma. "I am afraid I have forgotten where I left off."

"Grandfather had just requested to court you, and your brother Aubrey had burst into your father's study."

With a slight curve to her lips, the elder lady glanced to the side, and whilst her physical being remained in the room, it was evident she was lost in the memories she related.

---

1 Bodices of gowns were made with open fronts and the stomacher was the triangular centre panel used to cover the stays. It was either pinned to the stays or the bodice, or some had silk tabs to keep the stomacher in place.

Chapter 12

"Papa!" called Aubrey as he burst through the door.

"I am here, son. You have no need to yell so."

Her brother started when he noticed Rebecca and the earl. "Lord Matlock! I had assumed you had fled Marysden, determined never to return."

The earl stood and bowed. "Today's call began rather inauspiciously, though it has become more promising as of late."

Aubrey straightened and returned the earl's greeting. "Forgive me. I passed Sarah as she fled to her rooms. Mrs. Mallory explained she had locked herself in the parlour with the claim that you were trapped with her." Aubrey paused and glanced about the room. "However, you are here, so you could not have been."

Father closed the door before he replied. "Sarah, indeed, locked Lord Matlock within the upstairs drawing room, but Rebecca's quick thinking saved us a great deal of gossip and speculation.

"The earl has now requested my permission to court Rebecca."

Aubrey's wide eyes met hers, and she held her breath. What would he say?

"You have been acquainted for naught but a few days." His sceptical expression shifted from her to the earl. "Are you certain, sir?"

With a gasp, she stood and struck her brother in the arm with her fist.

"Ow! Rebecca! It is a legitimate question!"

Her father leaned forward upon his desk. "So it is, and one I was prepared to ask before your untimely interruption. I thought to request a moment alone with you, Lord Matlock, but

I suspect Rebecca will return to the servant's hallway and eavesdrop should I force her to leave the room."

"As would I!" interjected Aubrey.

With a shake of his head, her father sighed. "I hope you do not object, sir. Though I am certain they keep their own counsel at times, my son, my daughter, and I speak freely with each other."

Rebecca resumed her seat as Aubrey settled upon his usual corner of their father's desk.

"To be frank, my lord, my utmost concern is the rapidity of your courtship and the familiarity I witnessed earlier."

Lord Matlock made to speak, but her father raised his hand. "Please allow me to finish.

"I suspected some interest on your part when Rebecca confided in us your impulsive proposal upon delivering your sister's invitation to tea. It is now apparent that you have persuaded Rebecca to accept your suit, yet I wish to be certain you have considered the entire situation.

"My daughter boasts no connections of consequence and her dowry is a mere five thousand pounds—a pittance compared those of the Ton."

"Sir," interrupted Lord Matlock. "I am unaware if your son or Miss Rebecca has mentioned my late wife, as we have all had occasion to speak of her. The marriage was arranged by my late father and was not a happy one.

"I have no need of a large dowry or vast connections. I desire a wife who is honest, forthright, and takes an interest in myself, rather than my title or possessions. Since our first acquaintance, Miss Rebecca has illustrated each of these characteristics, and I find I wish to spend increasing amounts of time in her company."

Aubrey's eyebrows raised almost to his hairline, and he bit his lip, prompting Rebecca to clasp her hands in her lap and study them with fervour; however, she absorbed every word of the earl's complimentary remarks of her character.

"As I have understood matters, my sister has argued with you more often than naught."

Lord Matlock gave a rumbling chuckle. "She has, though we have spoken civilly of other matters. Miss Rebecca is intelligent and well-spoken, and she has no qualms speaking her mind."

"No, she does not," responded her father.

"I will grant consent for a courtship." Her attention left her hands and returned to her father. "You are the kind of man, indeed, to whom I should never dare refuse anything which you condescend to ask, yet I shall require you to wait more than four days hence to propose." The last was said with a hint of mischief and a curve of the lips.

Aubrey began to laugh, and Rebecca gasped at her father's tease.

"Papa!"

With a shrug, her father stood, rounded his desk, and offered Lord Matlock his hand. "If the earl wishes to marry into our family, he will have to accustom himself to our ways. He may as well know what he is about from the start."

Lord Matlock accepted her father's hand and wit with pleasure. Aubrey stepped forward and offered his congratulations to them both, pressing a kiss to her cheek before resuming his place.

Glancing between her father and brother, she cleared her throat. "What of mother and Sarah? Uncle is not likely to arrange for them to travel before the ball two days hence, and after Sarah's display in the drawing room, they will not step back and allow this courtship without protest."

"Your mother and Sarah shall have a convenient illness of some sort by the ball. Neither will attend. I am also appalled at Sarah's machinations and she will not be without consequences for today's shameful actions. Sarah will be confined to her bedchamber until I decide she has learnt her lesson.

"I could demand your mother remain within her chambers, but she is unlikely to do as I ask. Please be wary of her until she and Sarah travel to Chalfield."

"In light of your invitations to Lord Sudbury's fox hunting party tomorrow, might I suggest Miss Rebecca join my sister for the day? She would not be required to avoid her mother and sister, and I am certain Sophie would be delighted to have her company." Lord Matlock turned to her and raised his eyebrows. "Would that be acceptable to you?"

"If Lady Sudbury does not object to my call, I should be pleased to join her."

Her father's relief was evident, and the earl's shoulders relaxed at her assent. The earl was genuinely concerned at her remaining alone with her mother and sister at Marysden.

The clock on the mantel began to strike the hour, and he started. "I must depart in order to notify Sophie of her guest for the morrow. She will want to make preparations."

As he stood, Rebecca rose, yet still had to tilt her head upwards in order to meet his gaze. "Please tell Sophie not to make a fuss. I do not need any special consideration for the day. I will be content to spend the time occupied with whatever she is required to do. I do not wish to be an imposition."

A frown overspread his countenance. "You know very well that Sophie would never consider you an imposition, Miss Rebecca. If you recall, she had hoped for you to remain longer today, and will be excited by the prospect of your company during the hunt."

"If you are certain."

"I am quite certain." After a brief nod to her father, he held out his arm. "Now that we have settled that argument, I would be pleased to have you accompany me to my horse."

She placed her hand on his arm with a grin. "You have forgotten your way to the stable so soon? I was unaware I had agreed to a courtship with such an old man."

"Rebecca!" exclaimed her father in a scandalised tone.

Her lingering unease from the discussion about the following day dissipated at the sound of the earl's laughter, although, she jumped when, as they stepped outside, he leaned toward her ear.

"I remember well where I left my horse, yet I required some excuse to prolong my time with you." His proximity set her on edge once again.

She released his arm, skipped ahead, and turned so she faced him, walking backwards. "You have spent a prodigious amount of time in my company as of late, my lord. I read once 'Always toward absent lovers love's tide stronger flows.' Do you believe the poet speaks the truth, or does he give us nothing but pretty words?"

He reached forward and grasped her hand, forcing her to stop. "I could not say." His thumb traced a delicate pattern on the back of her bare hand and across her knuckles. She had forgotten to wear gloves. "What do you believe?"

The sensation was maddening and travelled up her arm. "I have never felt..." She cleared her throat. "That is to say... I have no such experience to lend my opinion."

His eyes studied hers as his lip curved into a contented smile. "I see." He lifted her hand and bestowed a kiss to the back before releasing it and walking past.

With a quick couple of steps, she was again at his side. "I am certain you could say whether you give any credence to the poet's assertions. Why do you avoid my initial question?"

His face gave no hint of offense as he peered at her from the corner of his eye. "I gave you a truthful answer. I simply could not say."

"You are impossible!"

"Forgive me for not providing the answers you seek, but I must return to Warrington." With one last soft kiss to her hand, he disappeared into the stables.

"Grrr!" she voiced in frustration. Her query was not that difficult! She simply desired to know if any woman had touched his heart. Why could he not give an answer?

With a whip of her skirts, she returned to the house, hesitating at the sound of the elevated voices of her father, her mother, and Sarah, which vibrated through the walls, and could be heard throughout the house.

She tiptoed around to the servant's hallway and the same corridor where she had stood with Lord Matlock, leaning against the wall as she listened.

"You would see Sarah ruined!" screeched her mother.

"I warned you before today, Prudence, I will not force any man's hand regardless of Sarah's ploy. She should not have attempted to entrap the earl and will pay the price for her actions."

"I will not miss the ball!" Her sister's voice was shrill and pained Rebecca's ear.

"You shall not attend, and that is my final word!" The tone of her father's voice was resolute and unyielding. Thank goodness he would not back down! "You have been warned time and again, Sarah. I have allowed your mother to indulge you, but I will not allow you to ruin this family's reputation. You shall remain within your chambers until your uncle's carriage arrives and you depart this house."

Sarah's tirade prompted Rebecca to silently groan. She had heard enough. Their arguments held no further interest, so she retreated to her bedchamber, pulled the pillow over her head, and muffled the sounds of their raised voices.

Chapter 13

As Rebecca opened her eyes, she gazed at the ornate canopy above her with a sigh. Sophie had not at all been averse to Rebecca's presence at Warrington the day prior, and had insisted she remain until after the ball—an invitation her father accepted without hesitation.

Though uncertain of the imposition, Rebecca was relieved. Sarah and her mother were both less than pleased with her father's plans and still knew naught of Rebecca's courtship with Lord Matlock. It was better they be uninformed of some matters, and Rebecca was certainly not opposed to being separated from the other female members of her family.

She pulled herself from the bed, wishing she could remain and laze the day away. Despite her reticence to rising, she donned her dressing gown, and pushed aside the drapery to view the weather. The sky was blue with a few white, puffy clouds, and the trees swayed a bit with a breeze. The day would be a lovely one!

Even though she anticipated the day ahead more now than she had a moment ago, a part of her was still uneasy. The manner in which she had left things with Lord Matlock still bothered her, and the day prior, the two of them had been unable to have any sort of a private discourse, catching glimpses of one another in passing rather than spending time within the same room.

The earl had spent a busy day with Lord Sudbury, Viscount Mappleton, and those of the neighbourhood who ventured to Warrington for the fox hunt, and the dinner planned for when the hunt was concluded—Sophie, Rebecca, and Lady Mappleton, Lord Sudbury's sister, dined together in the small dining room, the sound of the men's raucous laughter permeating through the walls.

Rebecca crossed her forearms over her chest and rubbed the upper sleeves of her dressing gown in an attempt to warm herself. She was about to return to bed when the door to the dressing room opened and Jane, Lady Sudbury's maid bustled in.

"Good mornin', miss." She set a small tea service on the table and opened the draperies before returning to the dressing room.

After taking the seat, Rebecca poured herself a cup of tea and had lifted it just short of her lips when Jane returned, several gowns draped over her arms.

"When you have had your tea, Lady Sudbury wished you to select a gown to wear to the ball."

The saucer clattered with the abrupt placement of the cup as she stood. "Whilst I appreciate Lady Sudbury's kindness, my gown was packed in my trunk from Marysden. I do not require the use of another."

The statement did not daunt Jane, who continued with her occupation. "I mentioned to my lady you have a gown amongst your belongings, which I suspected was for the ball, but she insisted you consider one of these."

Rebecca opened her mouth to protest, but the maid was too quick.

"I hope you will forgive me for speaking so, Miss Fairchild, but Lady Sudbury is hoping to ease your way with society. Lady Mappleton is a prodigious gossip. Her husband, the viscount, is a good man, but as a younger son, wed for money and position. The lady's dowry consisted of quite a sum as well as a sizeable estate. Her father even ensured he received a title after their marriage."

She bristled. "And Lady Mappleton will blather on that my gown is not fine enough?"

"Whilst your gown is very fine, some might use it to claim your family is not grand enough for Lord Matlock. The style and silk are not the quality of what is purchased in London."

Rebecca bristled. "How many will be aware that I have consented to a courtship with the earl?"

"Lady Mappleton is certain to have been told already, miss. Was the arrangement to be a secret?"

"No," exhaled Rebecca, "it was not."

The spacious bedchamber she occupied shrank until Rebecca felt stifled. She could not breathe! She needed to be out of doors!

"I require my habit. I should like to ride." The maid flinched at her tone, which was more abrupt than her usual manner.

Jane gave a brief curtsy. "Yes, miss."

Once she was prepared, Rebecca headed towards the stables with haste, striding with resolute purpose across the lawn, lost in her anger, until two hands grasped her upper arms. She gasped.

"Are you well?"

Her gaze was arrested by Lord Matlock who stood before her, an expression of concern etched upon his features.

"Release me."

His face blanched and his eyes held a myriad of questions she had no intention of answering at that moment. She required solitude.

"What has disturbed you so?"

Her head shook. "I want to go for a ride."

He offered his arm and gestured in the direction of the stable. "Then let us request the grooms saddle your mare."

Without taking his arm, she moved past and did not slow her step until reaching the stable, where Beatrice was requested at the first approach of a groom. The earl ordered his horse as well.

She scraped her thumbnail up and down the handle of her crop. "I should like to ride alone."

"You are aware that a groom must ride with you should I remain behind."

Her palm pressed to her forehead. How she wanted to strip the bark from the nearest tree with her crop! "I do not require a chaperone," she forced through clenched teeth.

"You are under Sudbury's protection. He will not think twice about releasing any groom from his employ who failed to see you off without an escort."

She suppressed the urge to growl in frustration. Why could she not do as she wished and be done with it?

When Beatrice was led forward, the earl helped her mount, but retained a hold on her reins until his own steed was delivered. Once he was atop the saddle, Rebecca cued her horse forward to a gallop, leaning forward in her seat and allowing the wind to whip against her face.

A backwards glance to ascertain if Lord Matlock followed was never necessary. The plodding of his horse's hooves could be heard at a matching pace close behind. He never rode alongside her or interrupted; rather, he remained nearby without impeding her need for solitude.

She pulled Beatrice to a stop at a small pond that bordered both Warrington and Marysden, dismounted and, after tethering her horse to a tree, walked along the bank. In the shade of a Weeping Willow, she stopped to watch two swans swimming languidly in the smooth, glassy water.

Footsteps came from behind, and she turned to face him. Her anger must have been obvious since he all but stepped back when she caught his eye.

"Will you not tell me what has you so disturbed?" he begged.

"Why does Sophie think so little of my father's ability to provide me with a proper ball gown? Do we lack taste, or is it simply our lack of money that she scorns?"

"Rebecca..."

A forceful hand pointed towards her chest. "My father took me to the local seamstress himself and requested the best silk

Mrs. Wilson stocked!" Her volume rose as she continued. "He allowed every indulgence she offered! It is by far the most beautiful gown I have ever owned—grander than what I wore to your sister's dinner!

"I am certain it is immensely suitable." Despite her ire, he did not raise his voice to match hers.

"Of course it is! And regardless of whether I wear a woollen sack or my best gown, society will still ascribe a myriad of improper explanations for us to marry, and they will always insist I should not be the wife of an earl!"

"A countess," he stated with a small smile.

"They are one in the same, are they not?"

With a grasp of her hand, he drew her closer, holding both of her hands as though they were a lifeline. "I have no care for such insipid prattle!"

"You cannot prevent it!"

"No, but I can give it no consequence. I can—no, not I—*we* can ridicule it for what it is—inane gossip! We can find humour in their lies and their idiocy!"

She shook her head back and forth. "You would not appreciate a wife who was an incessant object of scorn and contempt!"

A tug propelled her forward and a hand reached up to cradle her cheek. "Only in that it could cause you pain! I would never regret having you as my wife!"

She exhaled a long heavy breath, her fury dissipating at his soothing touch. "You cannot..." Her voice cracked, but she never finished since one of his arms encircled her waist, and his thumb brushed her cheek.

"I married a woman who was rich, titled, and had connections to some of the cream of society. Charlotte was the kind of woman I was expected to marry. Do you think she escaped their derision?"

He paused, but before she could open her mouth to answer, he began to speak once more.

"She still endured the mockery and gossip of certain ladies, although most courted her favour due to her title. Her family's status did not protect her as you might assume. It is inevitable. Who you are is of no consequence to those who spread their lies.

"I was miserable married to Charlotte." His face tensed, and his lip curled in disgust. "I shall not choose another wife based on society's asinine expectations. I have chosen you. I merely must wait until you are prepared to accept me."

She stopped and stared. Why was she so furious? Sophie would never intentionally wound her feelings! If she had not been so quick to anger, she might have refused Sophie's offer without such a childish tantrum.

"Rebecca?"

The sound of her name called her back to his earnest gaze. "I shall not allow anyone to harm you."

"You cannot make such a vow."

"I can, and I do. I wish for your happiness." He drew her closer, and she relaxed at his warmth and familiar scent. "I am in earnest. No one will cause you harm." His tone pled for her trust, but could she surrender herself so fully? "You must believe me."

"I want to," she mumbled into his coat.

He cradled her face in his hands and lifted it. "I shall prove it to you. Just give me time."

At her agreement, his heart, which had been pounding in her ear, began to slow. He brushed his lips against her forehead, and despite the impropriety, continued to hold her in his embrace.

"Will you tell me what caused such upset?"

After she withdrew to a more proper distance, she focussed on some tiny fish swimming close to the water's edge, uncomfortable confiding the reason for her ire. "I planned to wear the gown my father purchased for the ball, but according to her abigail, Sophie sent some of her older gowns so I could choose one more appropriate. I am certain her motives do her credit, but when Jane began to explain, I am afraid I allowed my anger to consume me. I needed to escape for a time, so I requested my habit and walked towards the stables."

"Which was when I encountered you?"

"Yes."

With a hand at her neck, his thumb lifted her chin to meet his eyes.

"I will wear the gown my father purchased," she stated with conviction and without one hint of hesitation.

His lips curved on one side, and he gave a nod. "I would never have asked you to do otherwise."

Chapter 14

When the earl and Rebecca returned to Warrington, Sophie met them in the hall, a worried frown upon her countenance. "Rebecca!" she exclaimed. "I am so glad you have returned! I believe we should have a talk."

"Perhaps I should refresh myself first." She brushed a hand down the flared base of her jacket.

Sophie gestured towards the drawing room. "Unless you are uncomfortable, I have no objections to your present attire."

With a glance at Lord Matlock, Rebecca entered, but upon the door closing, she and Sophie were not the only two people within the room. The earl had followed and taken a protective stance at her shoulder.

"A misunderstanding has occurred, Gerald. Hardly a matter worth your concern."

The earl took a step closer to Rebecca. "I do not doubt what you say is true, yet I will remain if it is all the same."

Sophie clenched her hands together before her with a nod as she turned towards Rebecca. "Whilst I did send gowns with Jane for you to consider, I had no intention of her belittling a piece you currently own, or for it to seem as though I did. Jane mentioned she had unpacked a gown she assumed was for the ball, but I was unaware your father purchased a new gown in anticipation of the event."

She sighed. "My primary concern, when I requested Jane deliver them, was that you might wear the same gown on the morrow as you did at the dinner party. Harriet... Lady Mappleton would deride that fact more than the quality of the fabric."

"I agree," interjected the earl.

"Then, you do not object to my..."

"No, dearest. Please wear what you wish! I only meant to help, not to slight you or your family in such a manner. Please accept my apologies."

Rebecca reached forward and halted the wringing of Sophie's hands. "Once I distanced myself, I knew you meant no insult. I merely required some solitude and time to think."

Sophie's shoulders had just relaxed when a knock sounded upon the door. She bid them enter, and the housekeeper poked her head inside. "I am sorry to interrupt, Lady Sudbury. Something has arisen in regards to the ball, and I require your approval."

After indicating she would be there directly, the countess's attention returned to Rebecca. "I wish I could remain and ensure you are well, but I must see to whatever issue has presented itself."

"Of course you must." She gave Sophie's hands a squeeze and relinquished them so the lady could depart. Sophie ensured the door remained open behind her.

"I was certain you had no need of my assistance, and I am pleased to find myself correct."

She pivoted to where the earl stood behind her, a smug grin upon his face. "With a sister as agreeable as Sophie, I wonder at your remaining at all."

"I had no doubts that this morning's debacle was a mistake of some fashion. I wanted to ensure the two of you had no further misunderstandings." He stepped forward and laced his fingers with hers. "I also vowed to protect you."

"From your sister?"

His warm, rich laughter followed hers, and with a tug of her hand, he pulled her a bit closer.

"Father?"

Rebecca wrenched her hand from his and stepped back. A young girl stood within the doorway, peering between her and the earl.

"Catherine!" Lord Matlock exclaimed with some surprise. "Where is Miss Preston?"

"We were to take a walk, but she forgot her parasol. I am supposed to remain within the hall until she returns."

"Ahh." He peered between her and his daughter. "Well, since you are here, I would like you to make this lady's acquaintance." His hand stretched in Rebecca's direction. "Lady Catherine Fitzwilliam, I would like you to meet Miss Rebecca Fairchild. Miss Fairchild, may I present my daughter, Catherine."

She curtsied. "Lady Catherine, I have heard much of you this past week. I am pleased to finally make your acquaintance." How odd to address a child in so formal a manner!

The child returned the curtsy, but with a look of appraisal that was beyond her mere seven years. "I am pleased to make your acquaintance, Miss Fairchild."

The words were congenial and polite, but they were empty. She did not mean them in the slightest.

"I should return to the bench." His daughter indicated a seat against the far wall. "Miss Preston will return in a moment."

Rebecca took a step forward before Catherine could depart. "I would take pleasure in speaking with you again. Perhaps we could enjoy a picnic one day soon?"

The child's head tilted with an air more befitting royalty. "I do not enjoy dining out of doors. I walk as my governess instructs, but I prefer to remain within the house." Whilst her tone had never been open and friendly, it had changed to become condescending.

"Catherine," her father stated without raising his voice. "You will offer your apologies to Miss Fairchild for your disrespect.

The girl's eyes moved to her father but did not hold any reverence or love within their depths. Instead, there were hints of resentment and derision.

"I apologise, miss."

"Oh! Lord Matlock! I hope she was no bother!" A woman, who appeared quite a bit older than Rebecca, hurried down the stairs and grasped the child's hand. "I told her to sit on the seat and remain until I returned."

"My daughter is never a bother, Miss Preston." His demeanour was genial, yet there was a mild rebuke laced within the statement. "As she was unsupervised at the time and likely bored, I am certain she heard my voice and sought me out."

"You are correct, of course," she agreed. "It shall not happen again, sir." The governess dropped a swift curtsy. "I will await you by the door, miss."

Lord Matlock dropped to one knee so he was face to face with his daughter. "On the morrow, we will take Miss Fairchild on a walk and show her our favourite places. Would you enjoy such an outing?"

Lady Catherine glanced at Rebecca and then back to her father. "It would be agreeable."

As he rose, the earl placed a kiss on his daughter's cheek. She showed no reaction to his affection or inclination to reciprocate it, but stood stock still until he stepped back.

"Will you come to the nursery before dinner?"

The hope that his daughter might show some enjoyment of his presence or time was evident upon his countenance, yet the girl was so formal and almost imperious. A weight settled upon Rebecca's heart as she witnessed their interaction. How sad!

"I shall, so you must decide which game you wish to play."

She gave a curt nod without a smile, and walked to the door where her governess awaited her.

When they departed, his smile faded, his shoulders drooped, and he gave a weary exhale. "I must extend my apologies for her manner. I have rebuked her time and again for her haughtiness, yet my words are for naught. She remains unchanged."

"You spend time with her before dinner?"

"I do." He stared with a wistful eye towards where his daughter left the house, then returned to the drawing room. "We play games, or I read from a book of her choosing. I pray one day she might hold me in some esteem. As it is, she feels no more for me than she does Miss Preston."

He appeared so crestfallen. "Perhaps, she is merely not an affectionate child? She may feel more than she displays."

A wan smile appeared upon his lips. "From the moment she first recognised her parents, Catherine showed a distinct preference for Charlotte. I still spent time with her in the nursery. It was how our tradition of games and stories before dinner began, but she never cared to be in my company as much as her mother."

"Lady Charlotte's death must have been difficult for her."

"She was so young." He sat upon the sofa and gestured for her to do the same. "I do not believe Catherine understood. I have tried, yet she requested to see her mother but a few months ago."

"How did you respond?"

The earl pivoted in her direction and extended his arm along the back of the furniture. "We gathered a few roses from the conservatory, and I brought her to the church where Charlotte is interred. Fortunately, her grave is along the perimeter of the chapel, so we placed the flowers upon the stone. I also helped Catherine light a candle and say a prayer."

Rebecca placed her hand upon the earl's wrist, causing him to give a slight jump. "It was a very kind thing you did."

"Charlotte and I may not have had a happy marriage, but I do love my daughter. I have tried." His attention wavered from her as if lost in thought.

Somehow calling him Lord Matlock or my lord was out of place. How would he feel if she…? "Gerald?"

His eyes snapped back to her face. "What did you call me?"

Her face burned and it took more than once for any sound to escape her throat. "Gerald." It came out more as a whisper. She bit her lip.

With a swift motion, he scooted closer and his large hand cupped her cheek, his thumb tracing a feverish trail up and down her temple. "Say it again."

"Gerald?"

He pressed his forehead to hers. "You are making my promise to your father impossible. Before he agreed to your stay at Warrington, he made me vow to adhere to propriety. A vow I am sorely tempted to break at this moment."

As he remained still, appearing to take pleasure in her presence, his eyes closed. Rebecca studied the curve of his lashes, which were long for those of a man, and then the shape and fullness of his lips. Oh, how she wished to feel them upon hers!

Before she could second-guess herself, she leaned in and pressed a soft kiss upon his mouth. She had never made any such promises to her father! The earl inhaled sharply in surprise, yet the sound made her stomach clench as her arms prickled with a chill.

His lips moved against hers, pulling at her top and bottom lip, before drawing back. "You should refresh yourself and dress for the day."

One long look at his eyes revealed his words were not a rejection. His feelings were there for her to see, yet so was the tension in his entire body. He maintained a tenuous hold on his self-control.

On impulse, she leaned forward and bestowed one last kiss to his cheek, rose, and departed. A glance back when she reached the stairs revealed he watched her as she left, and a prickling upon her neck told her that his eyes were still upon her, even now.

Chapter 15

Mary, who had been sent from Marysden to prepare her for the ball, secured the last bit of Rebecca's hair with a pin and stood back. "There!" As she stood, her maid shifted the seat and adjusted her skirt over the panniers. "You look lovely, miss!"

She ran the tips of her fingers over the white embroidery that decorated the pale blue silk of her gown. "Papa should not have spent so much."

"Well, if you'll pardon me for speaking, yes he should have!"

"Mary!" she exclaimed, shocked.

Her maid began to straighten, picking up the gown she wore earlier to put away. "Your father is a good man, but it is high time he overrode your mother!"

Mary was not usually so outspoken. Being at Warrington must have loosened her tongue. It was not as though her mother could hear Mary's remarks from Marysden.

"My father indicated my mother and Sarah are to depart on the morrow, so we will be free of her for a month complete."

A wicked grin crossed Mary's face. "Perhaps your uncle will find Miss Fairchild a husband, and your mother will choose to live with them. Then, neither would return."

Rebecca gave an amused snort. "I would not hold fast to such a notion. Sarah has not endeared herself to the men of this neighbourhood. It is only a matter of time before the eligible men of my uncle's society learn what she is about."

As she gathered the last of the mess, Mary stood straight and looked her in the eye. "I will still include it in my prayers, miss."

A giggle erupted from her lips at her maid's resolute nod at the end of her statement. Mary departed to her dressing room as Rebecca retrieved her reticule and took one last deep breath in an attempt to calm her nerves.

As she made her way to the grand staircase, she pressed her hand to her stomach. Why were the butterflies so persistent tonight? She gulped, but the squirming in her gut was still there.

When she turned at the corner, a hand reached out from the next hallway and pulled her down into the corridor. She gave a sharp inhale as she was drawn back against a warm solid body.

"It is me," Lord Matlock voiced by her ear. When the now familiar scent of cinnamon and cloves washed over her, she relaxed.

"Would it be so difficult to approach me rather than grasping me from behind?"

His low chuckle caused her to shiver when it rumbled across her flesh. With a hand to her waist, he rotated her within his arms.

"You are a bit pale." His fingers traced from her temple to her chin. "I hope you are not fretting about tonight."

She placed her hands upon his chest, her thumb tracing the trail of buttons upon his waistcoat. "I am nervous," she confided.

"You have no reason to be." He took a step back and appraised her new gown. "You are lovely. I shall be the envy of every man at the ball."

"You are a silver-tongued charmer, Lord Matlock."

"Only with you, Miss Fairchild. I have never tried nor truly hoped to court a woman until I made your acquaintance." His eyes spoke the truth of his words, at least the truth according to his heart and mind.

"What of your wife?"

His brow furrowed. "During our betrothal, I attempted to become acquainted with her but never felt the need for her approval as I do yours."

She bit her lip with a smile.

The sound of footfalls along the corridor startled them, and the earl withdrew to a proper distance.

He held out his arm. "Miss Fairchild, may I escort you to the great hall?"

"Yes, sir." She placed her hand near his elbow, but before he could steer her towards the stairs, Sophie's voice halted them.

"Rebecca!" The countess released her husband's elbow and hastened her pace. When Sophie arrived where she and Lord Matlock stood, she took Rebecca's arms, holding them from her body.

"Your gown is just lovely! I adore the white embroidery on the pale blue background. It is elegant—as are you, dear."

Lord Matlock nodded his head in agreement, though he made an odd jerking gesture with his head and widened his eyes at his sister.

Lord Sudbury laughed. "Do not forget your promise, Sophie."

Rebecca looked between the siblings. "What are the two of you about?"

With a giggle and a roll of the eyes, Sophie released one of Rebecca's hands and gave her a tug in the direction of her chambers. "I have something I should like to show you. Will you accompany me for a moment?"

She peered back at Lord Matlock, who had a soft smile playing about his lips.

"Sudbury and I shall await you ladies in the great hall."

The earls knew something, but what was it? Sophie tugged Rebecca forward before she could ask even one question. Inside the countess's bedchamber, Sophie retrieved a box from her dressing table.

"My brother brought me this yesterday in the hope you would wear it to the ball."

Rebecca frowned. "I do not understand. He could have given it to me himself."

"Until you are betrothed, it would be considered a rather extravagant gift. I have no doubt it will become yours before long, but for tonight, it is a loan from me."

As she took the box from her friend, she noted it had some wear, indicating it could be of considerable age. With a cautious hand, she cracked the lid and lifted it, gasping when she caught a glimpse of the contents. "It is beautiful!"

"Would you like to wear it?"

Rebecca reached in, and with a gentle touch, she traced the two strands of pearls nestled upon a bed of fine pink silk. She removed the necklace with care and draped it across her palm.

"Is it a family piece?"

"They belonged to my mother. She left them for Gerald to bestow as he wished."

Sophie could not have missed her swallow as she stared in awe at the necklace before her, yet it did not deter her. Her friend reached out, took the necklace, and unclasped it. "Turn so I can help you."

"But I could not possibly. What if I were to lose it?"

Sophie's chuckle was light as she walked around Rebecca to stand behind her. Once the necklace was in place around the base of her throat, Rebecca's fingers ran along from the ornate clasp at the back, discovering how the pearls were graded: here the pearls were smaller than those at the front, and a tiny seed pearl was set between each bead. They were exquisite!

"He wishes me to wear it?" She would be touching her neck all evening to ensure it did not disappear!

"He had hoped you would, and you are already wearing pearl earrings which match well."

She turned towards the mirror and took in her reflection. They did bring out the white embroidery in the pale blue silk of her gown, as well as made her appear more refined. She smoothed her skirt and placed a palm back against the base of her neck.

"Now, do not be nervous," scolded Sophie. "This is not an expensive piece when you consider the Matlock jewels."

An incredulous sound escaped her throat. "I do not know if I am fit to be a countess, Sophie." Her head and her body began to shake. "I never thought to be... I..."

Sophie clasped Rebecca's hands together between her own. "Do you care for my brother?"

Their eyes met, and Rebecca's vision blurred as she began to choke back tears. "I do. I am terrified by how swiftly my feelings for him have developed, yet I could not fight them."

"Do not fight them. They are what make you the perfect countess for him." Her words were so simple, yet how could it be so effortless? "Come."

Her friend tugged her through the corridors to the library where the earl had entertained her the night of the dinner party. Sophie led her before the fireplace.

"Do not move."

Rebecca made to step forward. "But..."

"I said do not move!" Sophie grinned and departed.

Where did she go, and why would Sophie leave her here alone? With a sigh, Rebecca pivoted in her spot, studying the room for an occupation whilst she waited. The door closed behind her, and her head whipped around to find Lord Matlock.

"Sophie indicated you were upset. I hope you are not displeased with the pearls?"

"No!" she exclaimed. "They are exquisite, though I fear losing them during the ball."

His lip quirked to one side. "Do not fret. Should the clasp break, I doubt they will vanish without your notice." He drew close and placed a hand upon her waist, his head angled so he could speak in her ear. "You have such a graceful neck. I knew they would be perfect for you."

She trembled as he dropped a kiss on the side of her neck along the trail of the pearls.

"You do not play fair." With a step back, she put some space between them in order to regain some equanimity.

He poured a glass of brandy and offered it to her. After she took two swallows, he finished the rest with one gulp and returned the glass to the tray. His large hand warmed hers as he lifted it to his lips, kissing her knuckles twice before trailing his thumb across the back.

"Do not fear me, Rebecca. I will do all in my power to ensure you have a happy life. Your trust will not be misplaced. I assure you."

"I do not fear you." Her voice was almost a whisper. "I do not understand why, but I fear the position I would take as your wife, the society, and my own feelings—but not you."

A knock sounded at the door but a moment before Sophie re-entered. "Are you well?" she asked Rebecca.

"Yes, thank you."

Sophie raised an eyebrow at her brother. "The guests should begin to arrive soon. Will you not join us?"

By placing the hand the earl never relinquished on his arm, Lord Matlock steered Rebecca into the great hall. Lord and Lady Sudbury remained at the entry with Lord and Lady Mappleton, but the earl guided her to the ballroom.

"Should you not be in the receiving line with Sophie?" The musicians were tuning their instruments, so they leaned towards one another to speak.

"I indicated a preference for your company. My sister did not argue."

She peered over her shoulder as she stepped out to the terrace. "Sophie has an agenda of her own, I believe."

With a frown, he followed, stepping around her to lean against the stone railing. "To my knowledge, she merely wishes to be of aid."

"Your sister cares for you and desires your happiness."

"She should not fret like an old woman." His voice held a bit of a dissatisfied groan. "Sophie is young and newly wed. She should not worry for me so."

Rebecca covered her mouth with her hand at his petulance.

"What amuses you?"

"You." She looked out at the garden in an attempt to rein in her amusement, but her eyes could not avoid him for long. They returned to his handsome face of their own accord.

"Me?" His eyebrows lifted as a lock of his hair fell from its ribbon to rest upon his cheek.

With a laugh, she placed her hand upon the railing, watching her fingers brush the coarse stonework. "Yes, you." She bit her lip and appraised him for a moment. "After your father's death, you saw to Sophie's debut, yet you did not welcome just any suitor when the gentlemen began to call."

He made to speak, but she raised her hand to stall him. "You waited until a gentleman who would appreciate her presented himself. Some brothers would have been eager to marry their sisters to any available man."

"They would be poor brothers if they neglected to ensure their sisters a good life."

"And you are amongst the best of brothers." Her scrutiny returned to her fingers. "It is only natural your sister would wish the best for you in turn."

"But you did not explain what was so humorous."

Her attention snapped back to him. "Did I not?"

"No."

"It is... it... it is merely that you were rather petulant when you complained of Sophie fretting over you."

"Petulant?" His voice was incredulous. As an earl, he must not be called as such often. "Are you saying I require a return to my short coat?"

An image of him in a young boy's attire came to mind and caused a burst of a giggle to escape from her lips. Her hand returned to cover her mouth.

With a grin, he stepped closer. His hand began to reach as though it might curl around her waist and render her light-headed again. He had not touched her, yet she could feel the strength of his hand against her side. She took a deep breath, waiting.

"There you are!" Aubrey stood in the doorway.

Lord Matlock's hand dropped to his side as he pivoted to bow in the direction of her brother and her father, who had stepped from behind his son. Her father glanced between the earl and herself as he reciprocated the earl's greeting and approached.

"You should not be without a chaperone." He did not hide his censure, but took her hand and placed it upon his arm.

"Footmen and maids bustle by the doors whilst they prepare, and the doors remained open. I saw no harm in taking the fresh air as we awaited the guests' arrival." The earl was even-tempered as he spoke, but it was clear he did not relish the scolding.

"My lord, you would run the risk of damaging Rebecca's reputation?" he replied, incredulous. "With the nature of my wife and eldest daughter, she can ill afford the local tittle tattle."

Lord Matlock stood straight and tall. His bearing spoke of his experience in standing before a group of people. "I have known your daughter but a week, yet there is no question in my mind of her becoming my wife. Whether the ceremony occurs within a fortnight due to an overzealous gossip or in several months' time because I require your approval makes no difference. Miss Rebecca Fairchild shall be the next Countess of Matlock."

Her face burned and did not stop with her cheeks. If the earl touched her cheek, his fingers were sure to be singed! The heat travelled down her neck and lit her chest from under her flesh. Aubrey's eyes were upon her, his brow lifted and his cheeks dimpled with the size of his grin. He would enjoy this far too much once she returned to Marysden!

The earl pivoted in the direction of the ballroom and held out his arm. "Miss Fairchild, shall we?"

With a heavy swallow, she glanced at her smug brother and her father, who did no more than tilt his head so he was appraising her over his spectacles. Before she could alter her resolve, Rebecca leaned forward to kiss her father upon the cheek, released his arm, and took the arm of the man her heart insisted she would one day wed.

Lord Matlock's facial expression may not have conveyed his delight with her actions, yet his eyes spoke more of his feelings than his lips or even his voice. As they passed through the doorway, his free hand covered hers, sending a frisson down her arm.

"Thank you, Rebecca," he whispered.

She bit her lip and held his steady gaze since she was too cork-brained to answer. Stammering and stuttering as she responded with some inane prattle would only mortify her.

A few guests now milled around the ballroom, and the earl swivelled to stand before her. "I have taken for granted that you will be my partner for the first set, which I must rectify immediately. Will you do me the honour of dancing the first with me?"

"Yes." Her voice was breathy and even cracked. What was wrong with her? She could not speak!

His dimple made an appearance as he leaned in just a hairs breath. "The supper dance as well?"

She attempted to clear her throat and still be ladylike. "I should enjoy being your dining partner, sir."

"Then all that remains is the last dance of the evening."

A high-pitched bark came from her before she could prevent it. "But that would be three dances!"

"And you will not dance with another man if I can help it," he growled. "My intentions will be clear to all and sundry by the end of this evening, Rebecca." His volume dropped when he addressed her with such familiarity. "If you do not wish for me to do so, then you need to speak at once."

He never wavered, but then, he never would. Her palms were damp and her heart thrummed in her chest, yet her entire being knew he was her future. It was why she had trusted him from the moment of their first acquaintance. "I would be pleased to dance the last with you."

His countenance bespoke of his pleasure, and all coherent thought left her brain. Darn that dimple!

Chapter 16

With a swift step, Rebecca descended the stairs and hastened from the house just as the clock in her father's study chimed quarter after seven. She would be late! The sun had made its appearance at the top of the hour, and she had promised so faithfully to arrive at sunrise.

Beatrice was saddled as requested, and once situated with her feet in the irons, she cued her mare to a canter. She could not travel too fast within the trees. It would not do to be whipped in the face by a passing branch. What a sight she would be then!

When she cleared the woods, he was waiting along the edge of the hill, Hermes stomping impatiently at the dew covered grass. Before he could approach, she brought Beatrice to a gallop and turned her east.

The sound of his stallion's hoof beats upon the ground gained as she rode further, yet he never attempted to ride alongside her. They had never ridden in that direction. Instead, they had always remained closer to Warrington.

The first fence was coming fast, and she gathered her horse for the jump. When Beatrice's back legs left the earth, she lifted her face. How she loved the feel of leaving the ground upon her mount's back!

She slowed when she reached the forest, and the earl upon Hermes drew up to her side.

"Where are you taking me?" he asked with a hint of a devilish grin.

"You will discover soon enough." Her teeth found her lip and began to nibble as she awaited his response.

His low chuckle made her smile, and she took a deep breath in an attempt to steady herself.

Weather permitting, the morning rides had become a habit since her stay at Warrington. The two of them could often be found riding the grounds of Lord Sudbury's estate or walking near the pond where she and the earl had argued prior to the ball.

The ball! That evening had changed her. She could not return to the girl she was—nor did she desire such a thing.

Gerald had lived up to his promise of not abandoning her to the wolves. He stood with her in the first dance, the supper dance, and the final set of the night. When she was not dancing with him, he introduced her to those of his acquaintance whilst he ensured she was never without refreshment.

A few of the gentlemen of the neighbourhood made as though they might approach her for a set, but the earl's steady presence at her side appeared to frighten them away. She could not say she objected to his manner since she enjoyed every minute of the ball.

His presence, however, was not of a possessive bent, which she would have protested within seconds. Instead, Gerald was clever, well-informed, charming, and capable of intelligent conversation. He was not simply good company; he was the best.

"You are quiet this morning."

"I overslept, and my father has often indicated I am not much of a conversationalist whilst I break my fast. I hope you will forgive me. I had not meant a slight or to ignore you."

He frowned. "I had no intention of my observation being taken in such a way. Please do not feel you should apologise. You never need request my pardon for being yourself."

She could not help but smile in response to his statement. He did not speak so to flatter her, which she appreciated. He was quite different from those she had met of his rank at Lord and Lady Sudbury's ball who complimented or praised, as though they enjoyed the sound of their own voice.

"Have your mother and sister adjusted to life at your uncle's estate?"

Rebecca chuckled. Upon her return to Marysden, Mrs. Mallory had detailed Sarah and her mother's departure as well as their plentiful objections to the journey, the discomfort of her uncle's coach, and her father's heartlessness for banishing them.

"According to a recent letter from my uncle, Sarah decided upon the announcement of their trip to Bath that she could forgive Papa for separating her from you." His groan prompted a grin.

"My mother's spirits have improved with the presence of eligible men for Sarah, yet she has not so much as penned a complaint to Papa."

"Your father did not seem discomfited by her silence when I spoke to him Friday."

"No, but my uncle has kept him informed of their safe arrival and health.

"Papa enjoyed the dinner at Warrington—particularly the port and cigars after dinner, though he will not tell me of the discussion."

The corners of his eyes crinkled as his lip curved to one side. "We took to teasing your brother of his intentions with Miss Abbot. The poor boy is besotted, but fears her feelings do not match his."

"Why will he not trust me? I have told him time and again how Emma favours him. She does not call at Marysden for simply my company."

Gerald's expression changed as he gazed at her with serious intent. "A man in love does not desire an unequal alliance. He would wish for the object of his affections to admire him with a fervour and devotion equal to his own."

The knot in her stomach indicated he was no longer speaking of Aubrey. He had yet to declare any deeper feelings since their courtship. Of course, he had spoken of his intention to make her his wife, but nothing of love had been mentioned. His regard and desire for her was evident in every touch and glance he bestowed in her direction, yet he was reserved when speaking from the heart.

Not ready to divulge more than he could discern by observation, she cued Beatrice to a canter, continuing at that pace until the trees cleared and the ruins of an old priory stood before them.

She pulled her mare to a halt, dismounted, and tied her to a small tree near the outside of the clearing. The earl followed suit and trailed behind Rebecca as she passed through the largest, centre Romanesque archway that still stood at what was once the front entrance.

"I had no idea this existed. I have never ridden in this direction before today." His voice held a hint of wonder, and she turned to witness him gazing up at the decoration of the stonework. He removed his gloves and touched the detail upon the wall. "I have seen a similar ruin once. It was rumoured to have once been a Cluniac priory."

With a nod, she stepped closer, whilst she freed her hands from her gloves as well. "My grandmother claimed it was such, but her information was from stories she had heard as a child. A fire is said to have destroyed the majority after King Henry VIII ordered the place closed and the land awarded to the Sudbury earldom. Time accomplished the rest."

"Do you often come here?" he asked, his eyes meeting hers.

"I enjoy bringing a book and reading whilst Beatrice partakes of the grass."

His dimple began to peek from his cheek. "Have you shared this place with another?"

She gave a slight shrug. "Aubrey knows of it, and we have ridden here. Though he has never dismounted and joined me as you have today."

His grin indicated her confession pleased him, but he remained in the same spot. Rebecca steeled herself, clenching her hands in fists to prevent them from trembling, and stepped forward one footstep at a time until she stood directly before him.

She was close, so close she could hardly draw breath, yet her eyes could not look upon his. Instead, they remained upon the buttons of his wool coat as she tipped up onto her toes and pressed her lips to his.

The sound of his swift inhale prompted gooseflesh to erupt down her arms as she gripped his sleeve with one hand. Her other sought a place upon his chest to steady herself. She pulled back but an inch, her lips reluctant to leave his as her eyes remained closed, uncertain of his reaction to her boldness.

"I love you."

Her voice was nothing more than a whisper, but he had no need for her to repeat herself. With a moan, he took possession of her lips in such a way that she leaned closer for balance.

She caressed his bottom lip between hers and an arm to her back drew her flush to his tall frame. His large hand to the nape of her neck cradled her head whilst holding her to him with a gentle pressure.

She had never been so secure yet so unsettled in her life. Her entire being quivered at the sensation of him solid and strong against her, her heart pounded upon her ribs, and all she could do was surrender herself and feel.

Her lips shifted to skim his once more, but before she could, his tongue slipped inside to stroke hers. With a gasp into his mouth, she repeated his motion as her fingers threaded through his curls to press him closer.

When the ribbon came loose from his hair, his locks fell free against her fingers as his lips left hers and travelled to the column of her neck. Her mind was such a muddle! A slight moan of complaint escaped upon his lips ceasing their onslaught where her shoulder and neck met.

His breathing was laboured, evidenced by his chest, which pushed closer with each heavy breath. Hers was no less affected, but in an attempt to calm, her shaky fingers combed through his loose locks, savouring their closeness whilst it lasted.

"You have shredded my restraint, Rebecca," he said, his voice rough and gravelly. A rueful chuckle vibrated against the sensitive flesh of her neck. "I became concerned after my outburst to your father the night of the ball, worried I had displayed a decided lack of respect for you and your father. I vowed that evening to limit my contact to what was proper.

"I do not want you forced to marry me, and I hoped to prove that I hold your reputation as dear as I hold you."

"You do care for me then?" The question was not unreasonable. He had never spoken outright of his affections.

His head lifted from her shoulder, an adoring smile upon his face. "You silly girl. Do you not know?"

She gave a one-shouldered shrug. "You have never spoken of your feelings."

Gerald's fingertips grazed from her temple to her chin. "My heart bound itself to yours when your eyes upbraided me on that hill for disturbing your dance. Since that moment, my affection has grown with every minute, every hour, and every day."

He cleared his throat as he fingered the bow upon the bodice of her gown. "When it became a deep, abiding love, I am uncertain. I was infatuated one moment and ardently in love the next. I planned to reveal my feelings when I proposed, but you anticipated me."

"I was decidedly improper to do so." She bit her lip as his eyes returned to hers.

"I have no care for your declaration being proper. To my ears, it was music from the heavens." A snort escaped and his brows lifted.

"Music from the heavens? Do you not think that quite mawkish?"

His dimple deepened. "I might take pleasure in showering you with oversentimental drivel." His head tilted to one side as he observed her for a bit. "I should woo you with one maudlin phrase a day—I believe when you least expect it would be best. Your reaction will make it worth the time it takes to compose such sentiments."

"You enjoy the ridiculous far too much, I think. You do realise father will not consent to our marriage just yet. We have been courting but three weeks."

He sighed and pressed his forehead to hers. "I may be more than ridiculous by the time I am allowed to take you for my wife." As if he made a great realisation, his head jerked back. "Are you saying you are of a mind to accept my hand?"

She backed from him towards what remained of a tower to one corner of the ruins. "Perhaps."

"Oh no, you will not evade my question, my love!" The earl lunged forward, and with a squeal, she ran. The manoeuver was futile since his long legs caught up to her under the archway. His long arm wrapped around her waist, and her back was pulled flush with his chest. "You should not tease me so."

Her breathing hitched at the feel of his warm breath against her ear. "You enjoy it."

He pivoted her within his embrace and held her fast. "I do, but it is unfair."

"Unfair?" she asked incredulous.

"Yes, unfair."

A burst of nervous laughter echoed through the remains of the tower around them. "How so?"

"For the reason that I cannot retaliate as I would wish until we are wed."

With a gulp, she attempted to quell the frustrating tremor in her hands. "Should I refrain from making sport of you until

Papa allows us to marry? I warn you. I do not believe I could prevent every quip from leaving my lips."

He swept a wisp of hair from her cheek. "I desire you to continue." Before she could respond, he bestowed a kiss to her lips and released them. "I will simply have to tally your offences against me and seek retribution after we are wed."

With a curve of her lips, she skimmed her hand across his chest. "I suppose I shall have to consider accepting should you ever make an offer of marriage."

A swift move had her lifted in his arms and pinned between the sheltered corner of the tower and his solid body. "Teasing woman!" His fingers reached under her arm and began to tickle, causing her to squirm and erupt into fits of laughter. The sound of his low rumble joined hers until he stopped, his hand poised for another assault.

"Would you care to reconsider?"

She bit her lip as she feigned thought, her eyes aimed up and to one side. When her attention returned to him, his expression was so light and happy it brought her joy. "Not particularly."

His fingers did not renew their onslaught as one might expect, rather he lunged forward and kissed her. Her senses reeled as his tongue immediately sought hers, and the hand under her arm skimmed across her breast.

Her body was aflame as his overwhelming heat combined with his attentions rendered her feverish. When his lips brushed along her neck, she shivered, and for a moment, before her eyelids closed of their own accord, the plants growing from between the stones of the ceiling were blurred above her.

Gerald gave a low, deep growl. His hips pressed flush against her, and his hand that supported her against the wall moved to cradle her rear.

How could he render her quivering and incoherent with a touch? The embrace of his body effected its own type of contact as the trail of his fingers and lips left a lasting impression, tingling long after he had moved them.

Her quick pants and his groans mingled with an occasional chirp of a bird until a neigh startled them apart.

The earl jerked back. In an instant, his eyes widened and appeared worried. "Rebecca, forgive me..."

She covered his mouth with her fingers as her feet were returned to the ground. "Please do not apologise. It implies you regret what we have done, and I could not bear it."

He cradled her cheeks in his palms as he bestowed a chaste kiss to her forehead. "I could never regret you, but I should not have lost control."

"My behaviour was no better." She glanced about the ruin. "Could we have been observed? The neigh?"

Gerald stepped around and peered out of their sheltered nook. "I believe it was Hermes. He does not like to be tethered for long periods of time."

"We should repair the damage to your hair." As she lifted her fingers to comb back his loose mane, he turned and closed his eyes, allowing her to bind his locks with the ribbon.

When she pulled the bow tight, he swivelled and kissed each of her palms. "Thank you."

"I suppose we should begin our return. Papa will send Aubrey to search for me if I am too long from Marysden."

His shoulders drooped, yet he did not relinquish her hand. With a gentle light pressure, he traced the tips of his fingers along the back and the tops of her fingers as if making a study of each small crease or freckle.

Once she freed one hand, she managed to retrieve her gloves from her coat pocket. "Gerald, it is you who does not play fair, now."

"If it affords me a moment longer in your presence, then I shall be exceedingly unfair."

She smothered her laughter in his topcoat as his body shook with the low rumble of his chuckle. She would indeed be late if the earl had his say!

Chapter 17

Upon waking to dull, grey clouds and an early rain, Rebecca shoved her face back into the pillow and grumbled. The fickle weather curtailed her morning ride and, by extension, her meeting with Lord Matlock. This was not a typical English shower, light and misty, but a steady storm that soaked the ground, rendering it soft and sodden.

As the dreary weather continued, she joined her father in his study where she read as he worked. From time to time, they spoke of inconsequential matters, returning to their occupations when they had quite exhausted the topic at hand.

Rebecca turned the page, but did not have an opportunity to read the first line before her father spoke. "The rain appears to have stopped."

Her eyes moved to the window. Would Gerald expect her to ride out as soon as the weather permitted? The ground was certain to be too wet for a good ride. She did not relish being atop Beatrice as she slid and slipped in the mud.

"So it does," she responded.

Papa scrutinised her carefully, but she could not hold his eyes, turning once again to stare out of the window.

"Should you not have Beatrice saddled in order to meet Lord Matlock?"

She raised her eyebrows at his astute assumption. "The rain was steady for some time. I am certain the ground is too soggy. Besides, I have no idea if Lord Matlock was to ride this morning."

A chuckle burst from his lips. "I am no dullard, my girl. You may not have expressed you were meeting the earl, but I knew what you were about."

She gave a huff. "For the most part, we only ride. I have taken him to one or two places around Marysden and

Warrington where we have dismounted, so he can view the area."

"Such as?" His eyes appraised her over his spectacles.

"I showed him the priory." It was a chore to keep her voice steady and even. She did not want to reveal the happenings of that morning.

"When was this?"

"Last week," she replied. "He was fascinated by the detail of the stonework." He began to laugh, and she bristled. "What is it you find so amusing?"

"Rebecca, you would be more proficient at concealing such personal matters if you did not blush as I question you."

With a snap, she closed her book and crossed her arms over her chest. "I cannot control that."

"Besides, you carried the faint smell of his cologne when you returned to the house."

Her eyes widened. "You never said a word!"

"If it were a common occurrence, then I would have reprimanded you both and demanded you marry with haste. However, I had not noticed such evidence prior to that day or since."

"Lord Matlock felt he was disrespectful at the ball when he indicated a forced marriage was not an unpleasant prospect. He has attempted to keep himself under good regulation, out of his regard for myself and his respect for you."

Her father leaned back in his seat. "He has mentioned as much to me, and I recognise that you both are human. As long as nothing occurs that will reap consequences." His brows were raised, and he appeared as though he expected an answer.

"I do not understand."

He shifted in his chair and rested his arms upon his desk. "Has your mother or Mrs. Mallory never spoken with you of marriage?"

"You are well aware, Papa, that my mother is insistent no man would take me for his wife. Mrs. Mallory merely refers to when I depart this house to live with my husband."

His hand ran through his hair and scratched the back of his neck. "I suppose if you are unaware of what I speak, then I need not worry. I should have a lady speak with you of such matters, though." He now avoided her eye and shifted once again in his seat. "Mrs. Mallory may not be the best choice as she has never been married."

"Perhaps Sophie?" Her father's awkwardness indicated the conversation he was alluding to would be mortifying should he attempt it. It might be embarrassing to ask Sophie, yet it could not be worse than her father, could it? "I am not betrothed as of yet. When matters are arranged might be a more appropriate time."

A knock startled them both, and they turned to find Mrs. Mallory standing at the open door. "I beg your pardon, but Lord Matlock has come to call." The earl stepped up behind the housekeeper as she moved to the side.

Papa jumped from his seat. "Lord Matlock!"

Did her father just mutter "Thank heavens!" before welcoming the earl?

Once their greetings were exchanged, Gerald sat in the chair beside her as her father resumed his seat.

"Did you tire of waiting for Rebecca to join you for your ride?"

The earl's brow lifted. "The ground is far too wet for a good ride. I did no more than travel here and Hermes' legs are covered in mud."

"So, no trip to the priory today?"

She rolled her eyes at her father's smug grin as Lord Matlock cleared his throat and shifted in his seat.

"No, sir."

Her father chuckled, and Gerald glanced at her, concern etched upon his features.

She shook her head. "Papa, please behave."

"I have said nothing for which I should apologise." He looked between the two of them. "I simply desire you to know that I am not as ignorant as one might think."

"I would never have assumed so of you, sir."

If only she could reach out and steady Gerald's hand, which now tapped on the arm of his chair. "We would be pleased if you could join us for tea." His eyes met hers and the rapping came to a halt.

"I would be happy to stay. If I could pen a letter to my sister, so she does not fret."

Her father pushed a piece of paper along with his pen and ink to their side of his desk whilst she stood. "I will inform Mrs. Mallory of the addition. Papa, when do you expect Aubrey to return?"

"He should return soon but shall require time to refresh himself." He turned to address the earl. "With the rain, we wished to know if the latest improvements to the drainage were successful."

Rebecca did not remain to listen to them speak of the drainage since she ventured down to inform the housekeeper Lord Matlock would stay for tea; however, Mrs. Mallory had already told the cook of the possibility, so Rebecca made her way back above stairs, passing a mud-splattered Aubrey on her return to the study.

"I saw Lord Matlock's stallion in the stable. Can he not go for more than one day without your company?"

She hit him in the arm. "He is staying for tea so please refresh yourself. I, for one, am hungry."

He rolled his eyes as he rubbed her target. "Yes, ma'am." A gleeful snicker came from him as he continued to his chambers. She would pay!

Upon her approach to the study, she smiled at the sound of Gerald's low chuckle to no doubt some joke or inane comment by her father. The gentlemen welcomed her when she entered, and it was not long before Aubrey joined them.

Tea with the three gentlemen was diverting, as all were possessed of good humour and intelligence. Over the course of their courtship, Gerald had become a part of their family. He genuinely cared for Aubrey as well as her father and had even accompanied them on occasion on rides around Marysden. His suggestions for issues with the estate were offered without fear of giving offense and were also taken with the utmost appreciation.

As they sipped from their cups, the earl's eyes often found hers, yet he proved time and again he was well aware of the conversation around him. Their gazes met as she peered out of the corner of her eyes in his direction. A flutter erupted within her stomach whilst she fought a grin. She could not give her father and Aubrey further mortifying topics for which they could tease her!

When they had finished their repast, they adjourned to the parlour. Lord Matlock had not been in that room since Sarah's attempt to entrap him, but he showed no signs of discomfort from that day. He claimed the seat that would make them partners as they played Whist and passed a pleasant afternoon in company.

When the clock struck five, the earl glanced up to the mantel as the last chime sounded.

"I should return to Warrington. Sophie will be expecting me for dinner, and I should like to visit with Catherine."

"Of course," replied Rebecca as she stood. "I shall walk you to the door."

After he bid her father and brother good-bye, she took his arm and accompanied him to the hall. As they stood hand in hand to bid one another farewell, a loud bang reverberated from the door, causing her to gasp and place her free hand upon her heart.

"Were you not expecting such a noise, my love?"

An amused smile upon his face, Gerald pulled open the door where a muddy and bedraggled man stood. The earl had no time to speak since the man stepped forward.

"I have an urgent express for Mr. Fairchild from Mr. John Whitney."

"What is it?" called her father as he descended the stairs.

"An express, Papa, from my uncle."

His forehead creased as he stepped forward to take the missive. The earl placed a coin in the messenger's hand, yet the man did not depart. He, instead, remained where he stood.

"I am to await your response, sir."

Rebecca turned to Mrs. Mallory, who had just entered. "Please see that this man is fed, and if we have them, please furnish him with some fresh clothes."

With a grateful nod, he bowed. "I thank you, miss."

"Dear Lord!"

Her father's exclamation diverted her attention from the messenger departing the room. "Papa?"

His hand rubbed across his mouth, and he exhaled as though a weight rested upon his chest. He struggled to master his emotions as he fixed his eyes upon her. "Your sister decided to attempt the compromise of a gentleman in Bath."

Her stomach began to churn, and she made a futile attempt to swallow the lump that had arisen in her throat. "Do not keep us in suspense," she begged.

"Unlike the earl, this man decided to take what Sarah so willingly offered with no compunction for their location or who might be about. Sarah, consumed with her own vanity, assumed he would be only too pleased to marry her, but the man has refused. He has ruined her without a second thought."

Her father aged before Rebecca's eyes as he moved to a chair along the wall and sat. "Your uncle begs me to travel to Bath. He has not abandoned his attempts to arrange your sister's marriage to this man, yet he cannot promise funds from me since he is unaware of what I can spare."

Gerald's hand covered hers, drawing her eyes up his arm to his beloved face. Her family was ruined! He would not... no, he could not offer for her now.

He had responsibilities and more than his feelings to consider. He may have intended to marry someone beneath him, but circumstances were altered. Her family, whilst troubled, was respectable when he requested a courtship. Now, those of their acquaintance would shun them.

Their association would ruin his daughter's reputation. His family's respectability tarnished if they did, indeed, wed. Her eyes burned as her entire being felt branded by her sister's shame.

She could bear it no longer! How could she listen to his dear voice explain why he must end their courtship—why he could no longer take her as his wife? They were not betrothed. There was no tacit engagement between them, and had they been betrothed, she would be obligated to free him. He could depart and never look back.

A sob rent from Rebecca's throat. Her eyes were blurred with tears. The warmth of a hand settled between her shoulder blades, but she shoved the attempt at comfort away. She could not lose all composure there before him! She would not have him feel guilt for an action he was required to take.

She propelled herself toward the stairs, taking them with haste as Gerald called her name. One of the men had attempted to grasp her arm as she passed, but to no avail.

The slam of her bedchamber door shook the house, yet she paid it no mind. With her hands upon her face, she collapsed upon the bed, her tears flowing freely as she heaved and sobbed into the counterpane.

Her body flinched when a hand rested upon her back, but it was too small for it to be her father or Aubrey's.

"There, there," crooned Mrs. Mallory. "I doubt it is so bad as you think."

She allowed Mrs. Mallory to take her in her arms and console her until Mary's voice brought her back to her surroundings. With a sniff, she made an effort to withhold her tears in order to hear the conversation around her.

"Mr. Fairchild and Mr. Aubrey are eager to be away. Only pack what Miss Rebecca will need for a day or two. We can send another trunk to Warrington on the morrow rather than prevent the master's departure."

So, Papa was departing for Bath. He would not make it far before he would be required to stop at an inn, yet he would arrive earlier than he would if he waited until the morning.

"Miss Rebecca, we need to put a cold towel on your face. Otherwise, you will be all red when you arrive at Warrington."

"No," insisted Rebecca as she rose to sit on the bed. "Can we not send a note to Mr. Abbot? We could say an illness in the family calls Papa and Aubrey to Somerset?"

Mrs. Mallory shook her head. "Matters have been arranged to the master's satisfaction. Lady Sudbury will welcome you at Warrington until the situation is settled in Bath.

"Lord Matlock was beside himself when you departed the room with such haste and insisted upon the arrangement. He wished his sister to be of use to you during this time."

"But I will be thrown together with him. How can I bear it?"

The housekeeper's eyebrows drew together. "How can you bear what, miss?"

"The earl has a daughter to consider. He cannot wed someone whose family is in disgrace. I cannot abide residing in that house with him, knowing he will be obligated to seek a wife elsewhere."

Mrs. Mallory stood and dampened a towel at the basin, wrung it out, and entreated Rebecca to lie down in order to place it on her face. "I could be mistaken, but Lord Matlock gave no indication he would cry off. He would have followed you to your chambers had your father and brother not interceded."

Gerald had never had the occasion to witness her in such a state. He would have been concerned, yet that did not change matters. As a father, practicality would be a necessity. She would be a luxury he could not afford.

A light rapping sounded from the direction of the hall, and a creaking indicated the door had been opened. The housekeeper spoke, but the individual words were not discernible.

Rebecca did not rise, but remained with her head upon the pillow. The cool, damp cloth upon her face soothed the irritation from her tears as well as tempered the pain that had begun to intensify in her head. She would be a mess when she arrived at Warrington.

"Miss Rebecca," called Mrs. Mallory. Her voice remained soothing, reminiscent of when Rebecca injured herself as a girl. "The carriage has pulled around front. Your father and brother await you in the hall."

She stood and brushed her skirts in an attempt to straighten any creases. Mrs. Mallory walked around her back, made a few tugs to her gown, and adjusted a hairpin or two.

"I will fetch your hat."

"Oh, please no!" Rebecca handed Mrs. Mallory the cloth when she turned. "My head is beginning to ache. I fear a hat will only make matters worse."

"You know you must wear a hat, miss, but I promise to leave the pins loose." After her nod, Mrs. Mallory helped her to don the wide-brimmed headpiece. The housekeeper grabbed a shawl from the dressing table and wrapped it around her shoulders as she guided her from the bedchamber. Rebecca allowed Mrs. Mallory to steer her to the front entrance where her father and brother did, indeed, await her.

Papa took her arm as he thanked Mrs. Mallory, and once they were inside the carriage, he squeezed her hand. Rebecca's eyes were heavy as she looked to her father.

"Did Mrs. Mallory explain that you are to remain at Warrington whilst we are away?"

Her head dropped back against the squabs. "It is very kind of Sophie to have me, but could I not stay with Miss Abbot?"

He shook his head. "Mrs. Mallory and Mary are the sole servants at Marysden who know the truth of our circumstances. I do not wish for the neighbourhood to ask too many questions." He sighed. "You will be better secluded at Warrington. Lady Sudbury will see to it."

She pressed her hand to her forehead with a whimper. Her head was beginning to pound.

"It will be put about that your mother and sister took ill, but you remained in the event the sickness is infectious."

Her eyes began to sting. How she wanted to weep and weep some more! She could not arrive at Warrington overwrought and with her face tear streaked.

Soon enough, their equipage pulled to the front of the great house, and they alighted. They were ushered inside where, after a kiss on the cheek from both her father and her brother, Sophie whisked her to a bedchamber.

Her mind was such a muddle, she did not listen to the directions Sophie gave to her servants. Instead, her friend combed out her hair and remained until Rebecca was prepared for bed. Once Rebecca was situated amongst the bedcovers, Sophie placed a small glass of wine into her hand.

"Drink this," she instructed.

With little thought, Rebecca drained the liquid and succumbed to the welcome bliss of sleep.

Chapter 18

Rebecca walked through the remains of the priory, a portion where, at one time, a stream passed through the structure. But now, only very wet weather saw this part of the ruin filled with water. As she gazed up at what remained of the once ornate walls and arched windows, she sighed.

Her stay at Warrington had not been what she had anticipated. In fact, for the past fortnight, Lord Matlock had not been in residence. The two of them had not been in company since the express arrived that fateful evening at Marysden.

Despite his absence, Gerald invaded her dreams nightly. No two fantasies were the same either. Each varied from nightmares of him informing her he could never wed into such a dissolute family, to feverish images of him kissing and caressing her in ways that prompted her to wake with a start, breathing heavily and trembling.

If only all her dreams were as comforting as the night she had arrived. That evening, his familiar scent of cinnamon and cloves surrounded her whilst he spoke words of love and adoration in his low reassuring voice. The tingling sensation of his lips upon her forehead, her cheeks, and her lips had affected her more than a mere fantasy. The dream had felt so real, and she could have sworn a hint of cloves remained, lingering in the air when she awoke the following morning.

A letter from the earl sat upon her dressing table, no doubt delivered by Mary at some time during the morning. She had slept late, and it was certain her maid had looked in on her prior to when she awakened.

The missive was opened with jittery hands. Would he end their courtship thus? In the stead of a rejection, a note of hope and love was read with eager eyes that put the words to memory and etched them upon her heart. If only time had not brought those niggling doubts that had festered and spread.

Rebecca had enquired as to his whereabouts, but Sophie would say naught but that he had urgent business that had necessitated his travel to London. He could not pen her another letter. The initial correspondence was decidedly improper—but then what about their courtship was in truth proper?

Her heart had taken a blow with each day he was absent and with every moment she was without word of Sarah's fate. Information from her father was vague and brief. He either had not the time to convey the happenings in Bath, or he was having poor luck in persuading the rake to uphold her sister's honour.

The disquiet that plagued her whispered that the earl wished for time to discover how her sister's scandal would tarnish the Fairchild name, or he wanted to see if her father and uncle could patch up the torrid affair. Regardless of the reason, his absence and lack of information eroded her hope as the rain and weather wore on the ruins before her.

How she desired Gerald's presence! Sarah had discovered a way to sabotage this just as she destroyed anything Rebecca held dear, yet Gerald was no mere gown or trinket. Her sister had torn Rebecca's beating heart from her chest and shredded it without a care.

In contrast, Sophie's presence and friendship had been a balm to her wounded soul. Her good friend made her excuses to callers, diverted Rebecca from her melancholy when it was necessary, and attempted to keep her busy in order to pass the time. Today, however, she was in no mood for company or false hopes.

Rebecca had dressed for riding and taken Beatrice across the hills before Sophie had ventured down to break her fast. She wished, for once, to indulge in the nagging fears and whisperings within her mind. It was nonsensical, but a facade was beyond her capabilities at that moment.

She whipped her crop at the long grass as she exited into the more open portion of the ruin. It was so frustrating to be left behind with no knowledge of the happenings a mere day's carriage ride from Warrington!

She stepped from the streambed and surveyed the clearing. The crumbled stone walls; a solid, tangible representation of her hopes and dreams. She had declared her love for Gerald here. A wry chuckle grated from her throat, and she brought a hand up to cover her eyes.

Strong arms wrapped around her from behind. With a gasp, she began to struggle, lifting her arm in an attempt to flay her assailant with her crop, but as her arm began its descent, a hand grasped her wrist.

"I would prefer not to be horse-whipped, if you are to take my opinion into account."

That voice! A loud cry pierced the calm whilst she swivelled in his embrace. "You are here!"

His dimple appeared as he gave a tired smile. "I have no other place I would rather be."

"I thought..." She stifled a sob, and he brushed the tears from her face with a gentle skim of his fingers.

"Did you not receive my note?"

She bobbed her head and took a trembling breath in an attempt to calm herself. "I did, but with a fortnight of little or no word from you or Papa—I began to worry matters were beyond repair."

His forehead wrinkled. "My business in London has kept me quite occupied. Have you not had word from your father?"

"He does not relate any news. His letters merely state he is busy with Sarah's predicament, he is pleased to receive my correspondence, and he is well. Aubrey adds a few lines at the end, but nothing of much consequence."

"I am grieved to hear the matter is yet unresolved."

She drew back. If he were to withdraw, she would be inconsolable. "I assumed you were corresponding with my father."

"The last letter I received from him was Friday last. I know he still had hopes of settling the situation with your sister, but I have not had word from him since."

Gerald's hand took hers and pulled, returning her to his embrace, one hand searing through the bodice of her gown at her lower back, and the other cradling her neck.

"Marry me." His eyes searched hers as her jaw dropped in shock. "I no longer wish to make polite conversation in the drawing room at Marysden or make clandestine arrangements to meet on horseback in order to spend time alone. My sole desire is to take you home to Matlock and to create a family. You, me, Catherine, and any children who happen to come along."

His cheek pressed to hers as his lips nuzzled her ear. "You only have to say yes, Rebecca.

She put a palm to each cheek and when she drew back, caressed his lips with hers. Their foreheads touched as she shook her head.

"You know I cannot."

His hands, which had held her as though she were made of delicate crystal tightened. "I know no such thing."

As soon as she managed to free herself, Rebecca retreated back to the streambed. Distance was a necessity. She could not think with him so close—with his hands upon her body.

She could not look at him and say what she must, so she kept her back to him as his footfalls approached from behind. "I would tarnish your good name. I would one day affect Catherine's prospects." Her voice cracked as she spoke his daughter's name. "I would prefer to remain in the dower house with my mother and Sarah than have you regret your commitment to me."

The earl took her hand and turned her around. "You silly girl," he said affectionately. "The memories of the Ton are not as long as those in the country. Whilst your sister might remain shunned here at Marysden, other scandals will distract London society from Sarah's ruin. In ten years, when Catherine is out, it is doubtful anyone will remember or care of an incident in Bath involving your sister."

"You cannot know for certain." Her voice was but a whisper.

"Oh, but I do." She gave a start, but allowed him to enfold her in his embrace. "Eight years ago, a young lady of good fortune and family was ruined at a London ball. She had two younger sisters who were shunned for a time after the eldest's indiscretion. The eldest was sent away. Rumours of a child abounded, yet there was never evidence to substantiate the gossip.

"Last season, the youngest of the sisters came out and was betrothed to a gentleman of good standing. The incident all those years ago received one or two whispers, but she still married well."

"What of the other sister?"

"She came out three years ago and wed a country squire, not unlike your father. I am acquainted with her father, who has informed me it was a love match."

"Both sisters are happy?"

His thumb brushed along her cheek. "They appear so when I have had occasion to see them." As he placed a kiss upon her forehead, he inhaled deeply. "Do not let your sister's situation impede our happiness. Your answer should be the desire of your heart alone without reference to your mother, your sister, or even your father and brother."

"How can I..."

"Catherine will not suffer for our marriage. I can only hope she will improve under your guidance. In ten years, very few will dredge up such old gossip. I assure you."

He clasped her closer. "I want nothing more than to be your husband. Can you not say that you desire to be my wife?"

With a hiccough, she sniffed. Her cheeks were damp with tears. "You *know* I wish for nothing more."

A groan vibrated his chest as his lips took hers in a kiss that demanded the final surrender of her heart. She ran her hands along his waist and gripped him to her. He was hers, and she would not let go.

Her tongue sought his and, for a time, their surroundings and their problems faded as she became consumed by him and his responses to their intimacy. Gooseflesh erupted up her arms when he gave a sharp inhale, and her stomach quivered when he moaned.

When his lips caressed the sensitive skin below her ear, she brought her hips flush to his body without thought. His hands cupped her rear and pulled her closer, yet no matter how tightly wound they became, they were not close enough.

Feather light fingertips traced along the top of her stomacher, leaving a scalding trail in their wake, as her high-pitched inhale brought his caresses to a swift halt.

"I forget myself when I am in your presence." He held fast to her as he buried his face in her neck, his breathing laboured. "I shall have to petition your father for a short betrothal. I cannot endure months of this."

She gave a throaty chuckle. "Will you expire from the deprivation, do you think?"

He bit with care where her neck met her shoulder, prompting her to gasp. "Take care. You will pay for your impertinence."

Gales of laughter erupted from her and filtered through the corridors of the ruin. "Then I shall be punished quite often for I am always impertinent." She placed a kiss upon his nose. "You prefer me thus."

"I do." His eyes were full of adoration as he looked upon her face. "I would never have you change."

"I am not fond of altering myself to suit others."

His dimple appeared. "I have noticed such a trait."

With a soft touch, she traced the lines of fatigue etched around his eyes. "We should return to Warrington. You require rest."

"If we return, I shall be required to share you. I wish to be selfish and keep you all to myself."

A deep neigh rang through the ruins, and she grinned.

"I believe Hermes is impatient to be leaving."

Rebecca took his hand and led him from the streambed, and to the large Romanesque arch at the entry where Hermes and Beatrice were both tethered to a nearby tree.

He tugged at her hand. "Rebecca?"

She entwined her fingers with his as she pivoted to face him.

"I was in earnest when I said I did not wish for a long betrothal. This last fortnight has been a misery. I missed you."

She trembled. "I have no desire for a grand wedding. I would want to be wed sooner rather than later."

He grazed his lips against hers and then, helped her mount. Once they were both in their saddles, they set off for Warrington, keeping their horses at a brisk walk until they emerged from the wood.

When she cleared the last tree, Rebecca gave him a grin over her shoulder and cued her horse into a gallop. The weight that had rested upon her for the past weeks was lifted. No more worry and melancholy consumed her. Regardless of the outcome of Sarah's predicament, her future was secure—she would not suffer.

He dismounted when he reached the stable, and after aiding her to descend from Beatrice, led her to the house.

"Accompany me to visit Catherine," he requested when they entered.

"You have not seen her for a fortnight. Are you certain she will not mind my intrusion upon your visit?"

With a shrug, he took both of her hands. "Whether she minds or not, she will need to accustom herself to your presence. You will be her mother soon enough."

"Do not refer to me as thus." His brow furrowed, and she squeezed his hand in reassurance. "I do not want her to feel as though I am trying to replace her mother. Her headstrong nature was apparent from the first moment of our acquaintance. I do not believe it will promote our relationship if she is forced to think of me or refer to me as her mother."

His eyes closed as his body gave an almost imperceptible slump. "You are correct. I have tried to prepare her for this day since it was inevitable as far as I was concerned. She may still be recalcitrant, though I would hope she accepts you straightaway."

"She will not if she feels pressured to do so." As no footman was present in the hall, she placed her palm to his chest. "I think it would be best for you to visit her alone today whilst I refresh myself, and I will await you in the library."

He removed her hand and kissed her knuckles. "Walk with me to the nursery?"

She took his arm and followed as she would follow him for the rest of their lives. As they climbed the stairs together, she nuzzled her shoulder against him whilst he bestowed a kiss to her crown. One last glance down to the hall revealed Sophie, who stood in the doorway of the mistress's study, grinning from ear to ear.

Chapter 19

The swishing of skirts roused Rebecca from reading as Sophie dropped onto the sofa across from her.

"Why will you not let me help plan your wedding?"

Rebecca laughed at Sophie's pout and, after marking her place, closed her book. "Papa has not yet approved of our betrothal much less a date. I shall wait until he returns and can have his say."

Her friend gave a frustrated huff. "It will not hurt to look at fashion plates for a gown or consider a menu for the wedding breakfast. Might your father allow me to host the breakfast for you?"

"I am certain he will be pleased to allow it since my mother would not condescend to do so, and if you held it at Warrington, she would have no opportunity to attend."

Sophie's pleased grin prompted a shake of Rebecca's head. "You may plan what you wish, but do not count upon a specific day. My father may not agree to the date Gerald and I have selected."

Sophie wrinkled her nose. "If this business with your sister takes too much longer, you will be forced to move the wedding to January. A Christmas wedding would be lovely! The house would be decorated with garlands and holly for the season as it is."

She held out her hand to halt her friend's plans before they became too ambitious. "I have indicated you could begin planning the wedding breakfast, but we have no wish for a large celebration. We would be pleased to have merely family attend."

"You know that will not do," Sophie tutted.

"My betrothed shall have what she desires, Sophie." Gerald entered the room, placing a hand upon Rebecca's shoulder when he stepped beside her.

As she tilted her head, Sophie smirked. "You should mind your familiarity with Rebecca. I doubt Mr. Fairchild will be as understanding as I have been."

"Speaking of Mr. Fairchild," he said as he placed a letter before her. "This arrived as I was passing through the hall. I hope it is the news you seek."

Rebecca's eager hands grasped the missive, broke the seal, and unfolded the paper with haste.

> *Trim Street, Bath*
> *4 November*
>
> *Dearest Rebecca,*
>
> *It is with great relief that I can report your sister was wed this morning in a small ceremony at St. Swithin's here in Bath. This must come as quite a relief to you, and I beg your forgiveness in not keeping you informed whilst your uncle, brother, and I attempted to bring this marriage to fruition. Though, now that the deed is done, I am at liberty to lay the details before you without fear of bringing you grief.*
>
> *Upon our arrival, the gentleman who had thus far refused to wed Sarah, a Mr. Beresford, was still adamant he was not obligated to her. We increased her dowry and made threats of which he, no doubt, knew we had uttered out of sheer desperation. The abominable young man appeared to find the entire situation amusing, with little or no care for Sarah's future.*
>
> *Your mother was beside herself. She blamed me for sending them to your uncle and your uncle for bringing them to Bath—with no admitted culpability on her part. I am certain you shall roll your eyes as I do when I consider her view of the scandal, yet I have every belief that when the two of you meet once more, she will invent some aspect for which you shall hold blame. Forgive me, but I cannot think well enough of her to hope for better.*

Meanwhile, your sister was a different creature than the one who departed Marysden. I was told her first reaction had been to rail against Mr. Beresford, and that she dissolved into hysterics when it became clear his refusal was in earnest. Yet, as time passed, she became quiet and reflective.

Sarah and I have since spoken in detail of her mother and the past. I believe this experience has humiliated and chastened her, and I now worry for her future. I did offer to find an alternative other than marriage to such a man, yet your sister assured me she would accept the repercussions of her actions.

You must be all curiosity as to what brought this marriage to be; yet I know little of the particulars. A few days ago, Mr. Beresford appeared at the inn with none other than his father, who insisted upon a word with me. The elder Mr. Beresford had heard rumours of his son's exploits whilst in London and had travelled to Bath to ensure his son married Sarah.

I am uncertain how news of the scandal reached London, yet it has brought about the wedding. In this instance, I can only be grateful.

We will journey to your uncle's on the morrow to gather the remainder of your mother's belongings and should make our return to Marysden near the end of the week. I am pleased to hear of your health and improved spirits, and I am eager to affirm your words with my own eyes.

Affectionately,

Papa

She bit her bottom lip as she folded her correspondence. The gentleman's father heard of the scandal in London... in London.

"Is your father well?" asked Sophie, who observed her with concern.

Gerald squatted so he was at her eye level. "Has he managed to remedy the situation with your sister?"

Her eyes studied his as she continued to gnaw on her lip. He began to chuckle. With his thumb, he drew the flesh from her teeth.

"You will not require dinner if you continue as you are."

She removed his hand from her face. He would not distract her. "Why did you travel to London?"

His brow furrowed. "I beg your pardon?"

"Why did you travel to London?" She leaned forward. "Sophie indicated it was for business, but she never said of what sort. Were you required to visit with your solicitor?"

"It was business." His eyes shifted down as he attempted to take her hand in his. "A trifling thing really."

"A trifling bit of business takes a fortnight?"

"Rebecca..."

"You are concealing the truth from me. I am sure of it."

"My love..."

They both started when Sophie leapt from her seat. She stared at her brother as she shifted upon her feet. "I should allow the two of you a moment alone. The door will be left ajar, so be mindful of your voices."

With a rustle of her skirts, she was gone, leaving the door ajar a mere six inches.

"Sophie is aware of the nature of your trip to town. Why will you not share it with me? I am your betrothed, after all."

He stood and moved to the window, taking a great interest in what lay beyond the clear panes of glass. "You have not shown an interest prior to your father's letter. What has he written to cause you to question me so?"

She rose and joined him, handing him her father's correspondence. "Perhaps you should read it."

With a wary eye, he unfolded the page, then read it through. "I do not understand. This says nothing of me."

"No, yet Mr. Beresford's father heard of the scandal in London and travelled to Bath to remedy the situation."

As he passed her the missive, he regarded her incredulously. "And you believe I brought this to pass?"

"You must admit your trip to town was rather sudden. You had mentioned naught of it. I did not even see you—you hastened from Warrington before I awoke."

"Sophie indicated she had put laudanum in your wine, and I wished an early start. I could not have known when you would awaken."

She placed a hand to her forehead as her eyes blurred with tears. "I thought…"

His hand grasped hers and entwined their fingers. "What did you think?"

"I had so many thoughts. Had you left to distance yourself until you learned Sarah's fate? Did you intend to return?"

"I left a note with your maid. You claimed to have received it."

"I did, and I learned the day after your departure that Catherine remained at Warrington. Your words and her presence gave me hope, but you were gone for so long."

"It could not be helped."

"I am certain it could not, but the longer you were away, the more I doubted you would return. I read your letter over and over again to remind myself that you had not abandoned me, but under the circumstances and without your presence…"

He drew her a bit closer and placed a hand to her cheek. "I wished to pen another letter when I arrived in Town, which I thought to enclose inside my correspondence to Sophie, but before I left, she implored me to consider your reputation. Should the worst happen with your sister, we could not afford any hint of impropriety. We have thus far been fortunate; our displays of affection have not been discovered."

"Other than Papa."

"He would not spread such knowledge as gossip."

She sighed. "No, he would not." She studied him further as something niggled in her gut. He was telling a falsehood or hiding his business for some purpose. It had to be related to Sarah!

"Gerald, I want to know why you travelled to London. I do not believe it was just common business, but that you in some fashion intervened to help my family."

He pulled his hand from hers and walked to the fireplace, facing her with his hands out at his sides. "I did naught that could be considered important." His voice was raised, and his shoulders were tense.

"If you helped my family, it is important to me!" she cried.

"I did nothing for your family. What I did was for you!" With an abrupt pivot, he struck the heel of his hand against the hard, stone mantel.

"Much as I respect them, I believe I thought only of *you*." His voice was soft as he muttered the last of the words.

A determined stride brought her directly behind him, and she wrapped her arms around his stomach, pressing her forehead to his back. "But why keep it from me? Did you feel you could not trust me?"

"No, that is not so!" He lifted an arm so he could turn in her embrace. His hands cupped her cheeks. "I remembered the name Beresford mentioned by Lord Whitby, a friend from Cambridge. I could not be certain it was the same family, or if it was, whether I could effect any resolution. Whitby arranged a meeting with Mr. Beresford, who did turn out to be the father."

His palms caressed down her arms to take her hands. "The elder Mr. Beresford has been displeased with his son's lack of useful occupation for some time. Both the actions of your sister, as well as those of his son appalled him, yet he saw the situation as a solution to his heir's dissolute lifestyle. Before he departed, he indicated he would threaten to disinherit his elder son and settle his fortune upon the younger if a marriage did not come about."

"From my father's letter, his ploy was successful."

His fingers brushed an errant curl from her temple. "In the beginning, I did not inform you of my plans in the event I was unsuccessful."

"I would have appreciated your attempt," she interjected.

A dimple peeked from his cheek. "Whilst I am sure you would be most grateful, I did not seek your gratitude, and I did not want your father to feel indebted to me."

She wrapped her arms around his neck and stood on her tiptoes. "My father need never know, but the next time we are alone, I *will* express my thanks."

"Rebecca." Her name was long and drawn out as if he was warning her.

With a gentle touch, she pressed her lips against his jaw before she kissed him. The door may have been open, but it mattered not. She would marry him on the morrow if someone insisted.

"Rebecca?" came Sophie's voice from outside the doors. "*Rebecca!*"

Chapter 20

Grandmamma tucked the blanket back from her new granddaughter's face with a loving touch. "Now that this wee one is here, where did I leave off?"

Elizabeth grinned as her husband hugged her close from his place behind her. "Sophie had entered to find you kissing Lord Matlock."

Her husband's low chuckle rumbled by her ear. "I knew you were not the usual lady of society, but this has been quite enlightening, Grandmamma."

"Oh hush, Fitzwilliam! I did not kiss every young man. The only lips to ever touch mine and that will ever touch mine belonged to Gerald."

"What happened after Sophie entered?" asked Elizabeth, fighting fatigue.

With a far away look, she smiled. "Well, in December, Gerald and I were wed."

Fitzwilliam scoffed. "I doubt it was so simple. Did my great-grandfather ever discover my grandfather's intervention?"

Grandmamma shook her head. "No, I respected Gerald's wishes on the matter. My father held guilt for Sarah's marriage for the remainder of his life. I would not pain him by taking the knowledge that he was of use to his family from him."

A glint in the old woman's eye drew Elizabeth's notice. "What became of your sister?"

"As penance for his dissolute behaviour, the younger Mr. Beresford was made to return to the family estate with his new wife." The dowager's voice cracked, but she managed to regain her control. "He resented her for being the cause of his banishment from London and Bath society and made her miserable for it.

"After five years of marriage, he fled for London and was shot by a peer who found Mr. Beresford bedding his wife. He did not survive the encounter."

Elizabeth's eyes burned with tears. "How terrible!"

"It was, but my sister rallied." The dowager's gaze returned to them with a glimmer not before seen. "You see, when Papa returned from Bath, he carried a note from Sarah with him, which apologised for her actions and begged my forgiveness.

"Papa felt she had truly changed, so I was willing to offer an olive branch. I responded, granting her forgiveness, and began a correspondence, which lasted through the turbulent years she was wed. When she was widowed, she came to Matlock and stayed with Gerald and me for the time of her mourning.

"She and Sophie were both at my side when Anne was born. Sarah became a most devoted sister—though Sophie was always wary of her."

"Did Sarah ever remarry?"

Elizabeth rested her head against Fitzwilliam's broad chest, which vibrated as he spoke.

"She did. Gerald's cousin visited whilst travelling between London and his estate in Cheshire. He became taken with Sarah and returned often until he could garner her consent for a courtship. Once they became better acquainted, she fell in love with him, and they were wed but a few weeks after she came out of mourning.

"Charles was a good man, and he was as devoted to her as she was to him."

Elizabeth was shifted when her husband gave a start. "You do not mean Aunt Sarah, who passed nigh on five years ago?" A curve of the dowager's lips answered his question without words. "I heartily disliked her during your story, and I have difficulty reconciling the woman I remember with the girl of your childhood."

"My sister was quite altered after Bath. She learned the lesson my mother failed to recognise with her own ruin. Mr. Beresford was not a husband worth appreciating, but to Sarah's knowledge, father saved her reputation by arranging her marriage. I spent the time following Beresford's death convincing her that her treatment at his hand was not deserved—she felt it penance for her misdeeds."

"What of your mother?" Elizabeth's voice was groggy and her eyes heavy.

With a sigh, Grandmamma smoothed her skirt. "My mother wished to remain with Sarah, but the Beresfords would not have her. She returned to Marysden with my father and Aubrey.

"She resented my betrothal to the husband she wanted for Sarah. My sister's husband, whilst wealthy, was not a peer and was worth five thousand per annum."

"A respectable income," observed Fitzwilliam.

"It is, though I always believed she was angered more because I made the better match." An annoyed grimace crossed the dowager's face. "She did believe she had a right to appear at the wedding and take her due as the mother of the bride. When my father informed my mother the week prior that she would not attend the actual ceremony, she was incensed. Sophie's refusal to admit her to Warrington for the wedding breakfast made her unbearable.

"My father decided that since I was betrothed, he would move forward with his plans to install my mother in the dower cottage. He had intended to move with her to minimise the gossip, but Aubrey and I would not have it. He sacrificed too much. We would not see him abused for the remainder of his days.

"Aubrey requested the hand of Miss Abbot as soon as my mother was settled in her home. They were married the following spring."

With a hand to the mattress, Elizabeth shifted. She could not fall asleep until she heard the entirety! "Did your mother ever find any measure of contentment?"

"I do not know. She fled Marysden two years after Aubrey's marriage. When he reviewed her books, Papa believed she was hiding money from her account to afford the escape.

"We hired men to search for her, but she had vanished. After the time period required, he had her declared dead."

A grin lit the old woman's face. "I know he never intended to remarry, but he made the acquaintance of a lovely woman several years later. She was a companion at the time to an elderly neighbour—a spinster, who he enjoyed the company of immensely."

"He deserved some felicity in marriage," observed Fitzwilliam.

"That he did." Grandmamma's expression was still amused with one side of her lip curved upwards. "This time, his move to the dower house was voluntary. He and Amelia desired their solitude.

"Their only sorrow was that Amelia had found herself with child twice but lost both not long after they quickened. The midwife believed her age was to blame.

"Gerald and I sent them on a tour of Italy after the loss of the second. Aubrey ran Marysden, so Papa and Amelia had no obligations. Sarah and her husband sent them to Ireland two years later."

Fitzwilliam's arm held Elizabeth a bit more snug against him, his arm supporting hers that held their new daughter. "I find it odd your mother never sought out Sarah after the death of Mr. Beresford."

"My mother attempted a correspondence with Sarah not long after her marriage to that man. Sarah penned a copy of her response and enclosed it within a letter to me. She took her mother to task for her treatment of Papa and me. Sarah also wrote that she would not have attempted to compromise Beresford or Gerald had my mother not pushed her so.

"Sarah informed mother that she would have naught to do with her whilst she was so vindictive."

"That letter must have come as quite a shock," exclaimed Fitzwilliam.

"Indeed! My mother railed against my father for turning her beloved daughter against her and burned the missive."

Elizabeth's vision darkened, and she started as Grandmamma leaned forward to take the baby.

"Lizzy, you can scarcely keep your eyes open. You must rest."

"I want to hear all of the story." Her voice was weak.

Fitzwilliam pressed a kiss to her temple. "Grandmamma is not departing. She will be at Pemberley for as long as you have need of her. You can ask her any questions you wish over the upcoming weeks."

"My grandson makes a good argument. You will be tired of my tale if we continue."

She handed her daughter to her great-grandmother. "I shall never find that story dull. I assure you." With a hand to Grandmamma's arm, Elizabeth halted her movement. "You and the earl had a deep, abiding love and an obvious attraction to one another.

The elder lady blushed and straightened as she cleared her throat. "I am unsure I want to comment upon such a statement."

Elizabeth grinned. "I am merely surprised you only had two children. I am aware it happens, but I am amazed you did not have more."

A shadow passed over Grandmamma's face. "Gerald and I believed we lost two babies before Henry, one between Henry and Anne, and one a year after Anne's birth. We could never be certain since none of them quickened, but I had all of the signs."

"I am so sorry, Grandmamma."

The elder lady's time-weathered hand took Elizabeth's. "We were devastated with each loss, but in time, we came to terms with it. I had such a fever after the last that the midwife and doctor believed I would never have another child. They were correct."

Elizabeth made to speak, but Grandmamma anticipated her. "I feel we cherished Catherine, Henry, and Anne more than had we not had those losses. They were spoiled with attention, and we never travelled without them.

"Do not be grieved for us, but allow that they influenced us to be different than most peers and their children. We gave Anne a different upbringing, thus Fitzwilliam was raised more by his parents than his nursemaids and his tutors.

"And if you consider, it has influenced how he desires his children to be reared. You are allowed to be the mother you wish because of the choices Gerald and I made all those years ago."

The ache in Elizabeth's chest ebbed away as she gazed at her daughter. She never would have considered it from such a perspective.

Grandmamma grinned. "I do not mean to imply you would not have prevailed upon him to oppose convention."

With a giggle, Elizabeth snuggled a bit closer to her husband. "I would have fought quite the battle, but I am pleased it was not a necessity."

Grandmamma rose, pressed a kiss to the baby's forehead, and placed her in the cradle, tucking the bedclothes around her until she was snug. With a proud expression, she studied her great-granddaughter.

Overwhelming fatigue prompted Elizabeth to finally close her eyes. Fitzwilliam caressed her shoulder and down her arm as she sighed in contentment.

"You have never mentioned her name."

The voice roused Elizabeth, and she opened her eyes. Grandmamma stood in the same spot, but her brow was furrowed.

"Rebecca," Elizabeth said softly.

Grandmamma's eyes welled with tears as she placed her hand upon her stomach. "Rebecca?"

"Yes," responded Fitzwilliam. "Rebecca Jane Margaret Darcy."

"Oh!" She made her way to the side of the bed where the sound of her bestowing a kiss to Fitzwilliam made Elizabeth smile. "You honour me by giving her my name. Thank you."

Warm lips pressed against Elizabeth's forehead. She opened her eyes as Grandmamma placed her palm to Elizabeth's cheek. "I know how you esteem your sister. I am humbled that you included me with her."

"I love you, Grandmamma."

The dowager rose with her hands in front of her. "Enough of this! I love the both of you, but I will not cry!"

Fitzwilliam chuckled, provoking his grandmother to point in his direction. "Do not laugh!" Her husband only laughed harder.

Grandmamma huffed. "I will inform your father of Rebecca's birth, so Elizabeth may rest."

Elizabeth's eyes drifted shut as the click of the door latching closed reached her ears, images of Gerald Fitzwilliam and Rebecca Fairchild invading her dreams.

One could not deny that the earl's conquest to win Grandmamma's heart was a romantic tale. In time, it would become one of Elizabeth's favourites—one she would tell to her children and grandchildren.

The only story to surpass it in her heart would be that of Fitzwilliam Darcy and Elizabeth Bennet.

About the Author

L.L. Diamond is more commonly known as Leslie
to her friends and Mom to her three kids. A native of Louisiana,
she has spent the majority of her life living within an hour
of New Orleans until she vowed to follow her husband to the
ends
of the earth as a military wife. Louisiana, Mississippi,
California, Texas, New Mexico, Nebraska, and now England
have all been called home along the way.

After watching *Sense and Sensibility* with her mother,
Leslie became a fan of Jane Austen, reading her collected works
over the next few years. Pride and Prejudice stood out as a
favorite
and has dominated her writing since finding Jane Austen Fan
Fiction.

Aside from mother and writer, Leslie considers herself a
perpetual student. She has degrees in biology and studio art,
but will devour
any subject of interest simply for the knowledge. As an artist,
her concentration is in graphic design, but watercolor is her
medium
of choice with one of her watercolors featured on the cover

of her second book, *A Matter of Chance*. She is a member of the Jane Austen Society of North America. Leslie also plays flute and piano,
but much like Elizabeth Bennet, she is always in need of practice!

Leslie's books include: Rain and Retribution, A Matter of Chance, An Unwavering Trust, and The Earl's Conquest.

Acknowledgements

I have to thank Jane Austen, whose timeless works have inspired me and others to re-imagine her unique and beloved characters into countless scenarios as well as times. She had a talent few possess for words and though she meant them to be more satires than romance, I appreciate both aspects when I read one of her wonderful works

Huge hugs and thanks to Lisa Toth, Kristi Rawley, Suzan Lauder, and Janet Foster who have spent their free time pouring over, critiquing, and correcting these chapters. Their hard work helps make this suitable for reading! As we say on the boards, all mistakes are mine!

I would like to thank those who run and frequent the JAFF forums, especially A Happy Assembly and Darcy and Lizzy. You have provided me a launching pad for my work and helped me become a writer—a life I never dreamed I would have. I appreciate the support of those who comment and leave me feedback as well as the community itself. Your support has meant a lot!

I would like to thank the ladies and gent at Austen Variations for welcoming me this year. The more I become acquainted with them and meet these amazing authors, the more I find to admire about them. They are wonderful people and colleagues. I still have to pinch myself at times that I am included with such company.

I miss my mom every day and wonder what she would say at my writing. She always encouraged my creativity. I had just about any art or craft thing I wanted when I was a child. She introduced me to piano, bought me my flutes, and fussed when I didn't practice. She also never denied me a book and introduced me to Jane Austen. Mom! I thank you and I love you!

Lastly, I have to mention my family. They roll their eyes at the mention of Jane Austen, Pride and Prejudice, or sometimes

Persuasion, but have become accustomed to my obsession. My children brag that I am a writer and my husband has taken to chatting up my books in airports while he travels. He took vacation time to play the stay-at-home dad while I travelled to Jane Austen Regency Week and for a short trip to the Jane Austen Festival in Bath. He surprises me all of the time, and I know that when this book is released, he will make just as big a fuss as he did when I published the first. He is certainly amongst the best of men!

Lastly, I would like to thank everyone who bought a copy of one of my books. You make it possible for me to write! My muse thanks you as well!

When Elizabeth Bennet's parents attempt to force her into a marriage of convenience for the sake of her family, she flees to make her own future.

Will circumstances and their families conspire to keep Darcy and Elizabeth apart or will they unite to take them on together?

"A very refreshing and thought-provoking alternate path to Pride and Prejudice!" -Austenesque Reviews

"As with the usual 'what-ifs,' you can guess roughly where it is going and how it is going to turn out. However not with this book!" – My Kids Led Me Back to Pride and Prejudice

Single-mother and artist Lizzy Gardiner has just bounced back from a bad marriage when she meets businessman William Darcy; true to form, Darcy doesn't make the best of impressions. The problem is he finds himself attracted, but she is insistent on relying on no one but herself. Can the two of them leave their pasts behind and find love with each other, or will the ghosts of the past return to keep them apart?

"This is a unique take, with some excellent dramatic moments in typical L.L. Diamond style. It's not cut and dried at all, like most romantic writers, it's development is realistic and a bit raw." – Amazon reviewer

Two strangers with no one to turn to but each other...

Fitzwilliam Darcy is in a difficult situation. His father is pressing him to propose marriage to the last woman in the world he would wish to take as his wife. With a fortnight to announce his betrothal, he makes the acquaintance of Elizabeth Bennet, who is in a predicament of her own.

Could Darcy be willing to consider Elizabeth as a solution to his problem and to hers? And can Elizabeth ascertain enough of Darcy's character to trust him upon nothing but a first impression?

"I love a book that makes me smile, the characters were fantastic and it was so well written. I have read every P&P variation printed and when I come across a well written book with a fantastic storyline I can't put it down. This book was read in one sitting, I cleaned my teeth reading, and even cooked dinner reading, much to my poor family's taste buds or now lack thereof." – Amazon Reviewer

www.ingramcontent.com/pod-product-compliance
Lightning Source LLC
Chambersburg PA
CBHW061215170626
46809CB00003B/1361